SPIRIT of the SEASON

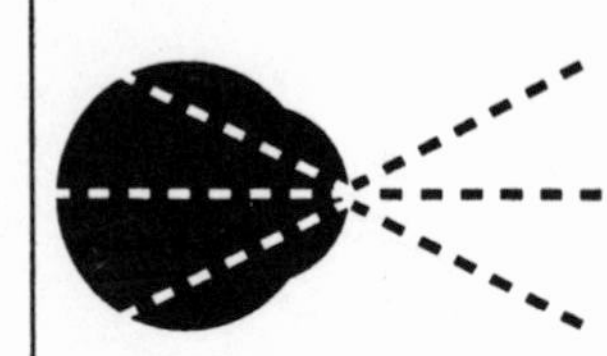

This Large Print Book carries the Seal of Approval of N.A.V.H.

SPIRIT of the SEASON

Heather Graham

Thorndike Press • Thorndike, Maine

Thorndike Large Print® Basic Series edition published in 1993 by arrangement with Dell Publishing, a division of Bantam Doubleday Dell Publishing Group, Inc.

Set in 16 pt. News Plantin by Penny L. Picard.

Printed in the United States on acid-free, high-opacity paper. ♾

Library of Congress Cataloging in Publication Data

Graham, Heather.
Spirit of the season / Heather Graham.
p. cm.
ISBN 0-7862-0050-2 (alk. paper : lg. print)
1. Large type books. I. Title.
[PS3557.R198S67 1993b]
813′.54—dc20 93-31462

Acknowledgments and Dedication

Dedicated to my agent, Mr. E. J. Acton,
the world's best, with special thanks
for his belief in this book.

To "Coach" Richard Murton, also the
world's best. And with special love to
Linda, his wife, and Monica, and Richie.

Now is where the dedication begins to read like a book itself, but after eleven years of the game, it could be no less. To the Coral Gables/South Miami Khoury League, without whose existence I might have spent a great deal more time writing and yet had much less to write about. To many more of the wonderful people we've met there, with whom we've yelled, hopped up and down, shared victory and defeat, and learned about patience, sportsmanship, baseball — and much, much more.

Here goes . . .

To Joe Garcia-Rios, Scarlet, and Kaila; the Holloways: Len, Ryan, and Danny; the Millers: Marilyn, David, Jason, and Aaron; Courtney Keller, Brian, and Cheryl; Judy and

Tony Rodriguez, Tony and Amy; Matey and Moe Veissi, Mal and Bruggie; Einor and Mary Pat Gustafson, Eric, Mark, and Carol; Jim and Dana Wiegrefe, Jamie and Brett; Jerry Rien; Brad and all the Nojaims; Hans and Laurie Huseby and family; John and Jane Knoppenberg; John and Donna Gazitua and the folks from Sergei's Cafeteria: Debbie and Jaime Ramires; Yvette and Tom MacKenzie; Will and Debbie Vespi; the Neales; the Courbiers; the Brennans; the Ferraris; the Sprouls; the Vaughns; the Fernandezes; the Tomayas; the Brewers; Father and Mrs. Tobin, Coach Palmer and so many more. In memory of Judi Griese and Lourdes Hassell, ladies who really knew how to support their teams. And for my own players, Jason, who could hit the ball, Shayne, who was always hit by the ball, and Derek, who continues to keep us all on the edge of our seats. For my one and only nephew, D. J. Davant, and his folks, Vickie and Davis. Last but not least, for "Papa," who came to every game he could, and for Nana Vi and Bill, who never fail to sit in the bleachers, cheering on the team, win or lose.

For Our '92–'93 Teams

The Blackfeet

Pat Hassell, Juan Pino, David Caldwell, Jeorge Smith, Antoine McLain, Javier Alvarez, Eric Gustafson, Omar Chacon, John Walpole, D'Angelo McIntosh, Derek Pozzessere

The Red Legs

Ricky Morad, Lazaro Valdes, Oscar Arias, Jaime Wiegrefe, Mark Naughton, Frank Valdes, Chago Hernandez, Aaron Miller, Brad Nojaim, Ryan Holloway, and Jason Pozzessere

Chapter 1

Becky Wexham exited her old maroon Volvo wagon, taking care not to smash the pink petals of her "Santa's elf" costume against the door. She usually changed from whatever costume — animal, vegetable, or mineral — she was wearing before heading home, but today Paige had called her at the mall to tell her that Mr. Beasely, the plumber, was waiting, and she had wanted to get home to talk to him just as soon as possible. There had been a time, she reflected ruefully, when she hadn't realized that being an "actress" would involve quite so many strange costumes — or that she would find herself stuck in them upon occasion.

But she had to deal with her plumbing problems quickly. Davey was at the park, trying to pretend that making the "Sharks," or the New Year's All-Star Team, didn't really mean anything to him, although she knew different. He always told her that he didn't really care if anyone came or not, that he just played ball because he liked ball.

But he *did* care. And he needed to be loved, more than her own kids right now. But first things first. Mr. Beasely was here. She had to take care of home.

She loved her house — even if it seemed to be decaying more and more daily. For one, she had bought it with Steven. Steven had been gone long enough now for her to cherish her memories without letting them cut into her too deeply. The house was a great big place. There were seven bedrooms, more than what they needed, even with Davey living with them now. They weren't huge rooms, but they afforded everyone in the house a little bit of privacy.

Maybe the parlor downstairs *was* a bit dark, but it was an old Victorian house, and the Victorians had been a bit dark and dreary. She had done the best she could with the dark woods, putting pleasant soft yellow draperies against them, and she had reupholstered the huge old Duncan Phyfe sofa herself in a similar material that somewhat brightened the space. At the moment, the parlor seemed very bright. She had gotten just a bit carried away with Christmas. They hadn't even gotten their Christmas tree yet, but the place looked like Macy's. There were lights hung all around the window frames, and a small set of them had even been placed around the big Christmas wreath over the fireplace.

Becky had always been totally involved in the spirit of Christmas. Even the year Steven had died, she had forced herself to put up a tree, she had brought the children to church, and she had tried very hard to hold on to the magic. It was a special season. Even in the most dismal of times, Christmas was the season of hope.

This year, it mattered more than ever. This year was for Davey.

And because of Davey, the parlor was rather strange-looking. There were all the Christmas ornaments — and then there was all of Davey's Babe Ruth paraphernalia: Dozens of books lined the old glass-enclosed law cases, while a picture of the Babe sat on top of the mantel, and an old poster on the wall. Paige was still groaning over the look of the parlor with all its lights and Babe pictures. Becky thought that maybe they had overdone the lights and the Babe Ruth stuff, but she knew what it was like to lose people, and if Davey needed to cling to the legend of an old baseball hero, then fine.

This Christmas, she was determined, would be good for all of them. But she was going to make it especially good for Davey.

No matter what Mr. Beasely had to say.

The front door opened as Becky started up

the short pathway to the house. Paige stood on the porch with Mr. Beasely.

Becky hoped Mr. Beasely wasn't going to charge her for the time he had been in the house, drinking hot chocolate, while he waited for her.

She fervently hoped that he was just going to tell her that she needed to get her septic tank pumped out. She could manage that bill by putting in a few extra days' work as an elf.

"My, my, Mrs. Wexham," Mr. Beasely said. "My, my." He was an ancient coot, by all appearances. He was bald on top, but long strands of snow-white hair stuck out at angles from his worn baseball cap. He was grinning from ear to ear, rocking on his heels, holding his mug of hot chocolate. He looked as smug as the Cheshire cat.

Her heart sank. There wasn't going to be minor trouble with her tank. The way he was grinning, it was going to be a big bill. A big, big bill.

"Hi, Mom." Paige grinned. "Cute outfit!" At fifteen, most of the time Paige looked as if she had stepped off the cover of a magazine. She loved clothes, and she loved makeup, and she was rather fond of boys, too. Becky felt a pang of sadness looking at her daughter. She was a beautiful girl, blond and blue-eyed like

Steven, tall, slim, and beginning to look very sophisticated.

She was also — when she wasn't at war with the boys — an angel.

Even if Becky had to dress up as elves and large tomatoes to keep it all going, she had long ago decided that she was a lucky person.

But now there was still Mr. Beasely.

And plumbing.

Becky wrinkled her nose at her daughter and looked anxiously at Mr. Beasely.

"What's the diagnosis?"

Mr. Beasely's grin turned into a big smile.

"It's shot right to hel— heck, Mrs. Wexham!" Beasely said, amending his word with a roll of his eyes toward Paige. "The whole system. Pipes, tank, leach field! Yep, the whole kit and caboodle. All of it. Everything! You name it! I do the works. Everything —"

"Everything. I think I've got that down now, Mr. Beasely, thanks," Becky said, lifting a hand to him. From the top of the porch steps Paige stared down at her sadly. "How much?" Becky asked from the bottom of the steps.

"Well, now." Beasely took off his baseball cap and rubbed his white head. "I estimate about five thousand. For you, I'll be doing my best to keep expenses down."

"Five thousand," Becky echoed.

"Well, that's what you'll owe me. I don't know what the tree people will want."

"The tree people!" Becky exclaimed.

"Well now, you see, you can't get back where the tank is, Mrs. Wexham. We're going to have to dig around the side of the house. That means taking down a few of the oaks. Of course, that means permits. But don't you worry none, the tree people will take care of what they need to. And I'll get the permit and all for the septic system. You don't need to worry your pretty little head at all."

Pretty little head.

Becky didn't see why he used the word *little* in relation to her. Like her daughter, Becky was fairly tall. Somewhere between five feet eight and five feet nine inches tall.

Thinking about the cost of a new septic tank, she could almost feel her burnt-auburn hair losing its color, strand by strand. There were going to be dozens of hairs, maybe hundreds, in new shades of silver.

"I've pumped you out, Mrs. Wexham. That should buy you a weekend's worth of time at least. If you go easy on the water." He pulled a card from his pocket. It was for a place called Jerry's Tree Service. "They're the cheapest and best in my book, Mrs. Wexham. They'll come and give you an estimate tomorrow morning, if you want. Call me about it. Let me know when you want me to start." He lifted his baseball cap to her and handed his cup to Paige. He walked down the steps, then winked at her. "That is a cute costume, Mrs. Wexham. Real cute."

"Thanks!" Becky heard herself say. She stood staring after Mr. Beasely as he walked to his big old truck and got in.

She stared at Paige again, her mind reeling. "Tough break, Mom," she murmured unhappily, biting her lower lip. "Hey, Mom, I can get a job after school this week —"

Becky waved a hand in the air, starting up the steps. "Paige, you have those college entrance exams right after Christmas, and you need to score high enough for a few scholarship offers." She reached the porch. "Besides, I think I've taken every available extra job there is in town." She grinned at her daughter. "Don't worry. Beasely just looks like an ogre. He'll let me pay on time." Five thousand. It seemed that half the country was out of work, but Beasely could cheerfully say the words *five thousand.*

Whoa.

She tried to dismiss her concerns and opened the door to the house.

Right on cue, the phone rang. "What do you want to bet it's Aunt Lizzie?"

It *would* be her sister Liz, Becky thought.

The way that the afternoon was going already, it had to be Liz.

News travels like wildfire in small towns. Liz would be on the phone demanding she sell the house, warning her that she had best turn Davey over to her care, and maybe a few of her own children, too. "It's a white elephant!" she would say of the house. "A monstrosity. Sell it!"

But Becky hadn't listened to any of the criticisms she had heard about the place, and she wasn't going to start now. It was perfect. It was big, it was comfortable — and it was the right place for her to raise the children, her own three and Davey.

Even if it was decaying bit by bit.

She stiffened her shoulders, ready to do battle. She saw Paige grin, and she grinned in return.

And she knew, come hell or high water, that she would manage to pay for that septic tank.

And make a few Christmas miracles, too.

There was a phone in the parlor, and she headed straight toward it. Without a pause she picked it up. "Hello, Liz!"

The moment's silence assured her it was indeed her older sister who had called. Dear Lizzie. They'd had an interesting family. Becky, at thirty-six, was the baby. Daniel, her brother, Davey's dad, had been six years older than she, and Liz, the eldest, had been six years older than Daniel. It seemed their mother had liked to send her children off to school before starting in with another baby. Maybe it was a good method, Becky thought with a shrug.

But now, she was left with Liz, staid and set in her ways as she closed in on fifty, who thought she was responsible for looking after Becky. Becky loved Liz — but she wished to hell that her sister lived in another state.

"What's falling apart in that old barn now?" Liz asked.

"Nothing is falling apart. I need a little plumbing work, that's all."

Liz sighed. "You must need all new pipes."

"Liz, please don't worry about it."

"I heard you were playing a tap-dancing Santa's elf over at the mall today."

Becky gritted her teeth. She counted to ten. "I had the time of my life, Liz! The kids are just great."

She could almost see her older sister's finger wagging at her. "But if you just had a normal job, Becky, you could pay for those new pipes."

Becky sighed. "We're in the middle of a recession, Liz. People with 'normal' jobs are being laid off left and right. I thank God I'm 'abnormal' enough to get a job as a dancing elf — it pays very nicely, and it also makes a lot of people very happy."

"You should send Davey to me. I can make it a better Christmas for him, Becky. You've got too much responsibility as it is. In fact, you should send your boys, too. Or maybe Paige."

"Liz, you come over here for Christmas dinner, just like we've planned," Becky told her firmly. Send Davey to her! Horrors! Daniel would roll over in his premature grave. He had loved Lizzie, too. But Becky and Daniel had been close. And they had always sworn to care for each other's children if something happened to one of them.

And it had happened to Daniel and Chrissy, his sweet young wife. A little landing-gear light had gone out in a 727, and the pilot had brought the plane down in a swamp. Only twenty out of the two hundred or so passengers had walked away. Daniel and Chrissy had not been among the twenty.

It was all in the past now. There was nothing anyone could do. Becky didn't blame God anymore. Not for Daniel and Chrissy, and not for Steven.

She just prayed that she could hang on. And she vowed that she would never, never give up Davey. She'd had him for almost two years now. She loved him with all her heart.

"Got to go, Liz!" she said suddenly. Davey — he'd be waiting at the park for her. The team meant so very much to him. There were going to be cuts today and more cuts next Monday. Becky wondered at the blundering intelligence of the league dads who had decided to form their final team before Christmas, cutting dozens of hopeful little boys. Not too many like Davey, not kids who had lost their parents recently. But she knew, too, that Little League had to work quickly — this was Florida. The season began in January and ended in May.

"I'll talk to you soon," she told her sister. "I promise."

"Wait!" Liz cried. "Becky, I want you to come to dinner alone here next week. I'm having over a friend, a man named Hank Weston, and he's been dying to meet you. He owns a whole chain of funeral homes, Becky."

If Becky had just been close enough to a wall, she would have been tempted to crack her own head against it.

The last thing she needed was a dinner date. And she could just imagine Hank Weston.

Her lips curled into a small smile. Right after Steven had died, over five years ago now, she had been in too much grief to ever imagine marrying again. But time had passed.

And just last year, she had begun an involvement with a really wonderful man. Handsome, fun. Bright. He had been just like a miracle.

But then . . .

Inwardly, she shrugged. She'd had a few dates before she'd met him, too. There had been Roger Burrows, the slick, handsome car salesman who'd called her relentlessly. He had a practiced sales pitch — for his cars, and for himself. He told her he loved kids, and didn't mean a word of it. She'd asked him in after their first date, because he'd insisted he really wanted to meet the kids. He'd smiled as if the curves in his lips were plastered on. Then he and the kids had all stared uncomfortably at one another until he'd finally sat down, but he'd managed to sit right where Paige had set her pizza plate — with the pizza still on it. His prize suit had been covered in olive oil, and the plastered smile had left his face as he muttered, "Damned brats!"

All right, they might not always be the best-behaved children in the world, but damn it all, they were hers!

And she hadn't been happy about going out with him anyway. She'd had a lousy time. In fact, she'd informed a tearful Paige later, the high point of the evening had been seeing him from behind, his perfectly pressed pants engraved with half-moon olive oil prints.

She'd almost laughed out loud; he'd been outraged.

Ah, well, no great loss!

Then there had been Paul Glover, an actor. The kids had hated him on sight. He, too, had insisted that he loved children. He'd spoken to them all as if they'd been infants — half-witted infants at that. She wasn't sure, but she thought that Jacob had probably been the one to put the frog in his glass of wine.

She tired of even attempting to date — families just didn't mix with romance. But then, almost accidentally, she'd met *him,* and she'd almost forgotten how badly things could go, because she had so much wanted things to work out. Wanting them to work out had made things worse. She had been a nervous wreck, trying to keep him away from her house, where all the disasters seemed to happen. He made it hard on her — he wanted to meet the kids. She'd learned enough by then to keep her family and her love life — if that's what you called it — separate. Time for the kids, of course, and time for herself and *him* too.

But things always happened with kids. She'd tried to arrange those private hours, and sometimes she did manage to see him, to have a wonderful time, but then . . .

She'd had to break too many dates. He'd never been married; his life was all in good order. He'd wanted to pick her up at the house, come into her home.

She'd been that route before.

And this man . . .

Mattered.

She'd been certain that had he actually come to dinner, he would have ended things instantly. Her home wasn't neat and clean and spotless, not like his life at all. Not that the kids actually threw food or anything — well, only during a real food fight at a picnic or the like — but they were kids, and the house was hectic, constantly full of their problems, and certainly filled with noise — the kids definitely loved to yell at one another. Yes, she'd found the most wonderful person — but not the one for her. He needed someone younger, say, someone single like himself, someone free, someone who didn't break dates constantly.

Breaking a date had been the final straw. Something had come up with one of the kids, she didn't even remember which one. He had been angry, insisting on knowing what was going on. And she had insisted that it was her own life. . . .

The whole thing had blown up into an awful argument, and he had walked away, telling her that she should call him if she really wanted to see him again.

And, of course, she'd never called. She could cope with the four children because she loved them so much. She could trip over balls and schoolbooks in the living room because she was a parent, and she'd learned to deal over the years with constant havoc. The doctor and dentist appointments were her responsibility, as were the meetings and the fender-benders and the strange things occasionally found in a little boy's — or a teenage girl's — bedroom. It wasn't fair to expect someone else just to smile and walk in on such a commitment.

She knew about being careful before she sat, lest there be a pizza plate beneath her.

She understood that Jacob had slipped the frog into the wine because Paul Glover had just been a jerk.

Better that they end it in a fight than that she learn to need him too badly, long too dearly to share all these lives with him, only to have him make excuses and slip out of the relationship once he realized that her life was burdened in a way that a single man might not want his to be.

And she couldn't bear losing a man a second time. He'd been too perfect. Too like a miracle for a widow in the latter half of her thirties!

It had been after this wonderful but quickly aborted affair that she'd paused to take a good look at things. Norman Cushy, the horticulturist who lived half a mile down the road, knew all about the many kids in her house, knew the place was decaying, and he still seemed to be enamored of her. But Norm had skinny little glasses that always slipped to the end of his nose, and though Becky was glad to be his friend, she couldn't see marrying a man whose BVD waistbands always rose an inch over his beltline. Norm was a sweetie and a friend.

But he wasn't, in the least, sexy or appealing.

The Norms of the world seemed to be all that was left for her.

Hank Weston would surely be another Norm. She couldn't take it.

"Hey, Liz, give me an early Christmas present, okay?" she said softly.

"What is it?"

"Don't fix me up for dinner with anyone. Okay? Promise?"

"Becky —"

"I've really got to go! It's getting late. I've got to be there for Davey."

Before Liz could say another word, Becky hung up firmly. She jumped off the couch, ready to run up the stairs to her own room.

"Paige, the roast is all set in the pan. Just put it in the oven in another hour for me, will you, please?"

"Sure thing, Mom. Oh, and tell that little butthead cousin of mine good luck, okay?"

"Don't call each other buttheads!" Becky called back automatically.

She didn't hear the reply. She was shedding elf petals and diving into a drawer for jeans and a T-shirt.

The sun beat down upon him. Davey Larson adjusted his cap. A cool breeze whispered by, but Davey barely felt it. He tried to give his entire attention to the enemy at hand — the pitcher.

It was Mike Harden. Davey hadn't seen any good reason to like a number of the boys in the league, but to his way of seeing things, Mike Harden took the cake. He seemed to think that he was a one-man team; not that he wasn't a good pitcher — he was. But he was such a jerk. Really, an A-one jerk.

It wasn't that he stood out there on the pitcher's mound spitting every other second as if he had a water faucet in his tonsils — a lot of the boys liked to do that. It was something in Mike's eyes. They were mean eyes, hard eyes. He didn't just like to strike out players — he like to make fools out of them.

His language was rough every time the coaches were out of earshot, and he was even nasty to his own teammates, allowing no room for error — for *humanity,* as Aunt Becky liked to say. Aunt Becky liked kids in general, but she didn't seem to be really crazy about Mike Harden, either.

Come on, come on, come on, Davey thought. It didn't matter if he liked Mike Harden or not. It mattered if he could hit the ball. He had to make the team. He just *had* to make the team. For Aunt Becky.

And there was Mike now, adjusting his hat, smirking away at Davey with his freckled face. Throw the ball, Davey thought.

He tried to think of the things the coaches told the boys when they were up at bat. Watch the ball, watch the ball. . . . watch the ball hit the bat. Keep the bat up off the shoulder. Watch the ball . . .

Then there was Coach Harden, Mike's father. "Hit the ball. kid. There's a buck in it for you if you do!" Sometimes he was worse. "Hey, kid. No pressure. But we've lost the whole game if you miss this one. Everybody's counting on you, kid. Come on. If you don't hit the ball, *you* owe *me* a buck!"

Hitting was Davey's weak point. He'd told the coaches when they were choosing the team that he could play first base, third base, or outfield. He'd done all right when the coaches had sent out pop-up flies and grounders. He'd caught everything he should have caught, and he'd made nice long, clean throws to first base, and back to home. He'd done okay running, too. He wasn't the fastest kid in the league, but he could get around. He knew when to steal, and he had the ability to pay strict attention to the coaches and steal when they wanted him to. He would do okay.

If he could just hit a good one. A really good one.

He just needed to get on base. A good solid hit that would get him on base.

Maybe it was because he needed help with hitting that he was so impressed with the Babe. George Herman Ruth, Babe Ruth. The man. Davey knew all about the Babe. He'd read everything ever written on him.

The Babe hadn't actually been an orphan. His mom had died when he'd been really young, but his dad had gotten to see him play pro ball. But he'd had trouble, lots of trouble, growing up. According to the Babe's own words in his autobiography, he'd started off as a "bad" kid, not really knowing the difference between right and wrong. So he'd been sent to a special school — not an orphanage, not a reform school, just a place for kids who needed help, and when he'd been there, he'd learned about baseball, and there had been a special brother there, Brother Matthias, who had seen his natural talent and helped him right along.

But he'd been able to hit. Just naturally. He could swing and hit the ball.

Even Babe Ruth had struck out sometimes. Aunt Becky had told him that often enough. He knew Aunt Becky wasn't really all that into baseball, but she'd read some of his Babe books for him.

And no matter what else was going on, she tried to show up at the park.

Mike Harden finally decided that he was going to pitch the ball. Davey could taste the orange dust of the field on his tongue. He could feel the sun beating down on him. And he could see the ball, a fast ball, soaring right to him.

He tightened up. *Watch the ball hit the bat!*

He swung. Swung hard and swung level.

The ball went whizzing by, right into the catcher's glove.

"Strike one!" the umpire called.

Funny how you couldn't even hear the ump if he decided to call a pitch a "ball." Umps just made little motions for balls. But heck, when it was a strike, the umps liked to make sure that fans could hear the call clear down in the next field.

He could hear parents, and some of the older kids, calling out their advice.

"Tighten up, Davey."

"Watch your feet, son! Step into the pitch!"

And there was Mike Harden. That blankety-blank-eatin' grin on his face. Mike Harden spitting — what did he have in his mouth, a bucket of drool? — and then winding up for the pitch.

The ball came.

Wide and high. It was wide and high. Davey held still.

The ump made his little motion. One ball, one strike.

Davey concentrated.

On the next pitch, he got a piece of it. As soon as the bat cracked the ball, he started to run. He was halfway to first base when the ump called "Foul ball!"

He trotted back to the batter's box, picked up his bat, and stared at Mike Harden. One ball, two strikes.

Then, out of all the yelling going on, he heard her voice. Aunt Becky's.

"You just need one, Davey! You just need one!"

Tighten up, hat off your shoulders. Watch the ball hit the bat. . . .

It was a bad pitch. He had a good eye — even if he couldn't always hit so well. He held dead still, and this time, he could hear the ump make the call.

"Too high." The ump shot up both hands, two fingers up on each. Two balls, two strikes.

One more ball came sailing by.

Full count. Now the ump waved a hand in the air with all his fingers, and his thumb knotted down. Full count. This was it.

"You can do it, Davey! You just need one."

If he just had some real help. Maybe just one day with the great Babe Ruth. The Babe could teach him how to hit a ball. He knew it.

He tried to think about the Babe.

I don't need a homer right now. Just a hit. Just a base hit to make these cuts. Just a base hit.

He concentrated with all his heart. Mike Harden threw again.

He heard the whack. He'd hit the ball. He started to run for dear life, waiting in the back of his mind for the umpire to call "Foul!"

But no one called out anything. From the corner of his eye, he could see that the third baseman had picked up his grounder. The ball was sailing in the air toward first.

He doubled up his efforts. Running hard, panting, his lungs bursting.

It was coming, it was coming. . . .

He picked up his whole body and sent it

flying over first. He made the curve away from the base just as the first baseman caught the ball.

He waited. Seconds that seemed like hours.

"Safe!" an umpire called.

Safe — by the skin of his teeth he was safe. But maybe that would be enough to make the cuts today.

"All right, Davey!" He heard Aunt Becky from the stands. He gave her a cheerful wave. She was standing right by the fence, her smile a mile wide. He nodded to her, a little embarrassed. It wasn't a real game, but he had to stay on base while Mike Harden tried to make fools of a few other boys. He was still being judged. He had to watch the base coaches, run when they told him to run.

Twenty minutes later, it was over. The boys in the tryouts, thirty of them today, gathered together in the field. Fifteen were to continue on.

Fifteen were to be let go.

To make things really worse, one of the coaches given the job of making the cuts was Coach Yeagher.

All the kids loved him. Tim Yeagher had spent five years playing pro ball, first with the White Sox, then with the Yankees. A car accident had nearly cost him a leg, and now he limped. He couldn't play pro ball anymore, and somehow he had wound up here in little Hampton City, central Florida, doing sportscasting for their local television station.

Tim was the whole reason Davey wanted to make the team so badly. And there was Tim, tall, with his warm smile, nice brown eyes, and sandy hair, trying to tell all the kids how he'd like to work with them, and surely one day he would. For the moment though, the boys who had made the cuts were . . .

Mike Harden. Right off.

Larry Appleby, Miguel Rodriguez, Billy Simpson . . .

Names. More and more of them.

Davey's heart began to sink.

Twelve names, thirteen names . . .

"David Larson, and Jeremy Richter. That's it, boys. For this particular team. But don't forget, we'll be forming our regular league teams right after Christmas, and everybody plays then. We've got great coaches in our league, so you all keep up your practicing through the holidays, okay? Thanks, boys, for coming out!"

That was it. Tim Yeagher waved and started to limp away. Davey unwound his legs — he had been sitting Indian style on the ground — and stood, still scarcely daring to breathe.

He'd made these cuts.

But would he make the next round, on Monday?

Aunt Becky was rushing up to him, her green eyes sparkling away. She offered him a fierce hug. "You made it!" she cried.

He nodded. He cleared his throat. "But there's another round of cuts. Next Monday, you know."

"Hey, one thing at a time!" she told him. She looked past him. There were a lot of kids and parents milling around.

Tim Yeagher was in the dugout, gathering up bats and base pads and batting helmets.

"Excuse me, just a minute, will you?" she said to Davey.

He nodded, watching her, his heart still beating hard. Becky walked over to the dugout.

Tim Yeagher was on the inside of the fence, and she was on the outside. Becky wound her fingers around the wire of the cage, and as Davey had, she cleared her throat.

"Yeagher!"

He looked up from dropping a bat into his green duffel bag of bats and bases. His brown eyes looked her over quickly.

"What is it, Mrs. Wexham?"

Becky bit into her lower lip. "What are his chances? For making the final cuts?" she asked softly.

Tim Yeagher shrugged uncomfortably. He didn't look at her for a minute, then his gaze fixed on hers. "I don't know. I honestly don't know. He *just* made these cuts."

Becky stiffened. "He can run like a deer! He listens to every word a coach ever says. He can throw —"

"And he's a weak batter," Tim Yeagher interrupted softly.

Becky gritted her teeth. The septic tank hadn't done her in, but this just might.

"He hit the ball today," she said, an edge of anger touching her voice. "I've seen all these kids strike out. I've seen great players strike out." She searched for more things to say. "Babe Ruth struck out now and then, and *you* struck out on more than a few occasions!"

Tim Yeagher stood straight, his hands on his hips. "Look, Becky, I want the kid to make the cuts! It's just that —"

"It's Christmas!" Becky reminded him. Jeez, she was ridiculously close to tears. "Some of these kids don't need — don't need magic this year. Davey does!"

Tim Yeagher sighed. He moved just a hair closer to the wire separating them. "Dammit, Becky, it isn't all up to me. There's a panel of five coaches! You know that. He's got a chance. He's got a fifty-fifty chance. He just needs to bat a little better at the next tryout. Okay? Listen, I've got to go. I've got to be at work in an hour."

Becky stared after him as he turned away. Davey was coming up to her, calling after Yeagher. "Thanks, coach!" Davey called.

Yeagher paused, waving a hand in the air. "Keep working all week, Davey. See you Monday."

Suddenly, Christmas music was blaring over the loudspeakers.

It seemed incongruous.

Merry Christmas — right, Becky thought. She looked up at the sky. Night was coming quickly. All around them, from the houses surrounding the park, lights were popping on. Red and green and golden, Christmas lights.

It was the season for hope, she reminded herself.

And she silently prayed. *Let the septic tank be bad! Let the whole place fall to the ground, let me play a tap-dancing elf until the world explodes! But, please, oh please, please, please, let Davey make this team!*

She smiled at her nephew. His eyes, green like his father's, green like her own, gravely stared into hers. She wondered what was going on behind that thoughtful expression.

She gave his shoulders a squeeze. "Let's go

home, huh? Paige put dinner in. It should be just about done."

He wrinkled his nose. "Paige made dinner?"

She laughed. "I fixed it — she put it in the oven. I'm not sure you've got a winner either way, but we'll soon find out."

He nodded.

All the way home, he was very quiet.

Silent, while the Christmas lights twinkled all around them.

Chapter 2

One of the really nice things about Aunt Becky's was that — even though it might be a crowded house with his cousins Justin, Jacob, and Paige — he did have his own room. If he'd been sent to live with Aunt Liz, he would have had his own room, too, and he was certain that Liz would have tried hard to be nice. But his dad had always said that Lizzie was an old maid with old maid ways, good at heart but maybe just a bit daft in the head. When his dad said that, his eyes would roll, and Davey knew that although his dad was fond of his older sister, he was also certain that life with her might be a fate worse than death. Davey's mother had been an only child, and his grandparents on her side of the family were very old, so Davey was grateful to be with Aunt Becky. He knew that things didn't tend to go so well for her, and though she would never let him go — never ever abandon him to live with Aunt Liz! — he felt sometimes as if he were another anchor weighing around her neck.

Becky was pretty. Not quite as pretty as his mom had been — no one was quite that pretty. He could even think that now without starting to cry. Maybe that was why he hadn't really noticed Aunt Becky a lot during the first year he had lived with her. He had been feeling sorry for himself, which, Aunt Becky had told him, wasn't such a terrible thing. He had survived a tragic loss, and he never should forget his parents.

He hadn't forgotten them. He never would. But he could see past things a little bit now, and he was worried about Aunt Becky. Coming back to his original musings, he thought again that she was pretty. Slim, with her red hair tied up in a ponytail a lot of the time, quick to smile, and always looking as if she cared very much with those bright green eyes of hers. She wasn't young, but she wasn't all that old, either. She was somewhere in her thirties. Late thirties, probably, but that didn't count. She hadn't hit forty — they hadn't had one of those "old buzzard" parties for her yet — so there still had to be hope.

She deserved something good in life.

And Davey was pretty certain that he'd found the "something good" that Aunt Becky ought to have.

It was Tim Yeagher.

Davey had started noticing Tim when he first came to town, around the end of the last season. Yeagher didn't seem to be terribly young — but he wasn't really old yet, either. He was a nice-looking guy, even if he did limp. And that didn't matter so much, because there were all manner of ways of limping — Aunt Becky was definitely doing a little bit of limping through life, too. Like Aunt Becky, Tim was real quick to smile, and he had warm brown eyes that twinkled and seemed to make his smile very real. All in all, Tim and Becky had all kinds of things in common.

They just didn't see it themselves.

Davey sighed and rolled over on his bed, staring up at the ceiling.

That was why making the team was so darned important. There would be dozens of practices and at least five all-star games against the nearby towns and cities. Aunt Becky would be at practice, and Tim Yeagher would be at practice. Eventually, they'd have to notice each other.

Not the limps, but the great smiles.

And all he had to do was make the team.

He might as well reach for the moon.

He threw his ball into the air, catching it back in his baseball glove. Then he set his ball and glove aside and stood up, walking to the old lawyer's case that served as a bookshelf in his room. He opened the top case reverently.

Out of all of his Babe Ruth collection, the piece he kept in the glass-enclosed case was the finest. It was rare. It was probably worth a fortune, his eldest cousin, Justin, had told him. He could sell it for big bucks.

But he would never sell it. Never. Not even if he were living out of trash cans or under a bridge. He'd keep it with him always.

It wasn't just a book, or a poster, or anything like that.

It was a cap. A baseball cap. One that the great Babe had actually worn.

Carefully, tenderly, almost as if he were touching fragile glass, Davey turned the cap in his hands. There, in the band of it, was the Babe's autograph: *Babe "George Herman" Ruth.*

The ink was beginning to fade just a little bit. Not that Davey touched the hat often. He knew that it was a rare collectible, and he loved to remember how it had come down to him. His grandfather — his dad's and Aunt Becky's father — had loved baseball, too. And his father, Davey's great-grandfather, had taken him to see Babe Ruth play. In those days, Davey's grandfather had told him, you could get close to the players. When a game ended, they had struggled and strained their way through the crowd just to touch the Babe, just to tell him that they thought he was great.

Out on that field, the Babe had seen Davey's grandfather. Just a little boy way back then, a very little boy, looking up at the Babe with all his respect and admiration in his eyes. The Babe had smiled. Not such a surprise. The Babe was supposed to have really liked kids. He'd had a hard childhood himself, and he'd always retained something special in his heart for kids. When he had seen the boy looking up at him that way, he had smiled big. A warm, wide, Babe Ruth grin. "Hey, kid!" he had said. "Did you like the game?" And Davey's granddad had barely been able to speak. He'd just stared at the Babe, a lump the size of an apple in his throat. He'd nodded.

The Babe had laughed. "Want an autograph, kid? No paper, huh? Well, we'll get you an autograph anyway!" He'd pulled the cap right off his head, yelled for anyone to hand him a pen, and then he'd signed his name, right in the cap, and tossed the cap to Davey's grandfather.

And so Davey had the cap now. He hadn't gotten it from his grandpa because his folks had died or anything — he'd gotten it years ago, just because he loved baseball so much.

It was his prize possession. He took care of it, he never brought it out just to show it around or to show off, and he was even careful not to handle it too often. It was a rare collectible, and maybe one day he'd want to give it to his own grandson. That is, if he ever decided that he wanted to get married.

If most girls were like Paige, he didn't think he would.

But then again, there was Aunt Becky.

He shook his head. His own future was a long way away. He had to think about Aunt Becky now. Aunt Becky with her plumbing problems and giant tomato costumes when she was doing restaurant promotions. Not that she seemed to mind working — she liked a lot of it. But he knew that last month she had wanted to turn down being a disco-chicken for the opening of a new fast-food restaurant. If she just had a little help in life, she could pick and choose when she worked.

And if he could just hit . . .

He stared down at the cap in his hands again, his eyesight just a little blurred.

"If I could just hit!" he said aloud. He looked up at the full-length picture of the Babe that he had taped to his bedroom door. The Babe was maybe thirtyish in the picture. Maybe closer to Aunt Becky's age. He was just a little paunchy around the middle, but his smile was there. That great, warm Babe Ruth smile. He was holding his bat up, high, off his shoulder. He was gazing at the camera, just as if he had been gazing at a pitcher. One like Mike Harden. Only the Babe's stare was challenging. Come on, it said. Give me your best, give me your very best. I'll belt it out of the park, right out of the park.

He'd been a natural batter. Yep, a natural.

But he'd worked at baseball, too. Hard. Davey knew that, because he'd read almost everything ever written on Babe Ruth. He'd read the autobiography the Babe had written with a sportscaster to help him, and he knew how the Babe thought. He'd had to work at baseball. He'd had talent, but he'd had to work, too. And he'd had great coaches.

Davey shook his head, staring at the picture on the wall. "I could do it, too. I know I could do it. If I could just have you with me once, Babe. Just once! You could teach me how to hit the ball. You could teach me how to point way far out into left field, and then belt the ball out there just like you did. If I could just have you with me. Once."

He stopped speaking and looked down, then gasped. He'd been so darned desperate in talking to the stupid picture that he'd squeezed the cap all up in his hands. He carefully smoothed it out and placed it back in the glass-enclosed case. He leaped back up on his bed, lacing his fingers behind his head.

Justin could help him, he thought dolefully. Justin was a pretty good athlete, and he was even fairly decent toward Davey, even if he did call him a butthead at times. But Justin had gotten a job for Christmas because Aunt Becky couldn't keep up all the insurance payments on the car. He was almost never around, and when he was, he was doing homework or playing around the basketball pole, since that was his main sport.

There was his cousin Jacob.

Davey wrinkled his nose.

Jacob never called him anything except butthead. Jacob wasn't quite two years older than Davey, and he was the least pleased of all his cousins to have Davey in the house. He wasn't bad, though, at baseball. He could have made the team himself, except that he was six months over the age limit for being on it. It was what they called a Midget team, and Jacob was old enough to be on a Juvenile team.

Yeah, maybe Jacob would help him. Especially if Aunt Becky asked him to. He'd be a real pest about it, and he'd throw baseballs anywhere but to Davey, but still, practicing with Jacob would be better than nothing.

"Kids!"

He heard the call from downstairs. It was Aunt Becky. "Come on down. Roast's on!"

Dinner. At least he'd get to tell Jacob that he had gotten this far with the cuts. It was better than nothing.

He started to open the door to run downstairs. He stared at the poster of Babe Ruth there.

He shook his head sadly. "If I could only hit! If I could just have your help once."

Oh, well. He didn't believe in Santa Claus, and he was plenty old enough to know that talking to a poster wasn't going to help him at all.

He hurried downstairs so that Aunt Becky wouldn't have to call up again.

Saturday at the market was a zoo.

Waiting in line behind what seemed like a dozen other shoppers, Becky wished that she had come in last night to do her shopping. But she'd been too tired after the tryouts and dinner and cleaning up, and by eight o'clock Friday night, she had convinced herself that she'd get started bright and early the next day.

What a mistake. Half the town had gotten up bright and early. And it was sure easy to tell that it was almost Christmas! People were being just as nasty as they could be! Christmas carols were blaring over the loudspeakers in the parking lot, but drivers were still beeping away, slamming on their brakes, and shouting "Jerk!" at one another just as violently as they could.

Once she had gotten into the store, a heavy-set woman had almost knocked her down over a particular head of lettuce. Another woman had rammed her cart right out of the way, and a red-nosed man had nudged her aside when the butcher had asked for her meat order.

Oh, yes. You could sure tell it was Christmastime!

It's going to be a *good* Christmas! she reminded herself. She stared down at her cart. She had several boxes of popcorn in it so that they could make popcorn strings to decorate the tree. She'd already told the kids that no one was going out tonight. They were going to have hot chocolate and popcorn while they threaded the rest. And they were going to play her Christmas albums even if albums were "archaic," according to Justin. She hadn't been able to afford a CD player yet, so they were going to listen to albums.

And they were going to love them!

It was finally Becky's turn. She winced when she saw the grocery total that rang up, and she made a mental note to thank the mall for that job as a tap-dancing reindeer.

She'd happily tap-dance her way through the mall again, and she remembered she was going to have to spend many, many hours as a pink-petaled elf to pay for the new sewer system.

Once again, as she drove out of the grocery store parking lot, she could really tell it was the Christmas season. People were beeping and honking as they vied for parking spaces. Apparently, she didn't turn quickly enough when she reached the street herself. A heavy-set man in a big old Cadillac behind her started to pound on his horn.

That was it. The wrong side of enough. Becky slammed on the brake and stepped out of her car. Her hands on her hips, she smiled sweetly as she came up to his window.

"Merry Christmas to you, too, buddy!"

He was so surprised, he stopped beeping. But by the time she was behind her wheel again, he was pounding on his horn again. With a sigh, she turned into the traffic.

What had happened to Christmas?

Maybe the chunky guy in the Cadillac had just learned that he needed a new septic tank, too.

She drove home, making mental Christmas notes. Another nice thing about her job as the dancing elf was that the entertainers had been counted as mall employees, so they had all been given ten percent discount cards for the mall. She'd been able to get Justin and Paige some great clothes and a basketball for Jacob at nice prices. She'd never really been very good at planning ahead, but over the past few years she'd learned to start early with the little "stocking-stuffer" sort of things, and so she was almost finished in that area. New socks for the kids, candy kisses, erasable pens — all kinds of useful little items helped to fill the stockings up. It wasn't easy. Liz had knit each child a stocking. They were adorable and unique, but very big. Smaller stockings might have been easier to fill.

She frowned. She was really all right on gifts except for Davey. There was only one thing that he really wanted, and that was to get on the all-star team.

He wanted on the team, and he wanted a signed Babe Ruth baseball card.

Even if she hadn't been up to her neck in sewage, she couldn't have afforded the card. The last she'd heard, there was one on sale somewhere in Miami for six hundred and fifty dollars — and that was supposed to be the deal of the century.

So what was she going to get him?

Especially if Yeagher cut him from the team. Yeagher had said he was a weak hitter.

She clenched her teeth, determined not to

think about it for the moment. This was Saturday. As it happened, there was no baseball. They were going to pop corn and have a good time stringing it.

But when she pulled into her driveway, the cheerful day she had planned appeared to be sinking right into the — toilet.

Mr. Beasely was back. He was walking around the yard with another man, pointing and gesturing. Becky stepped out of her car and hurried over to the two men.

Mr. Beasely was again sadly shaking his head. "Big bucks!" he was saying. "Big, big bucks!"

Becky paused. The men hadn't seen her yet. "Mr. Beasely, those big bucks have just got to start shrinking a little bit!"

Beasely swung around. He gave her his broad grin, as if casting her into a financial pit that rivaled the national debt were the high point of his Christmas season.

It probably was.

"Mrs. Wexham! This is Hal Cooper from the tree service, ma'am. I took the liberty of giving him a call, and he came down with me to take a look at things and see what I'd be needing. With the permits and all, we do have to start moving on this thing!"

Hal Cooper was younger than Beasely, but not by much. He was a stocky man, bald as a buzzard, and had bright hazel eyes that glittered the moment he shook her hand. "They've got to go, ma'am. This whole line of trees here, they've all got to go!"

She smiled, drawing her hand back. "And that's big bucks, too, right?"

Cooper grinned. He and Beasely looked just like Tweedledee and Tweedledum.

"Big bucks, ma'am. I'm sorry. Big bucks. We need the back hoe, the grinder, and all kinds of spit and hard work."

"What kind of big bucks are you talking?"

"I reckon two to three thousand."

She gasped out loud. Didn't they know there was a recession going on?

Behind her, someone cleared his throat. Still reeling from Cooper's estimate, she swung around. A young man stood there, maybe eighteen, thin and dark-haired and looking very uncomfortable.

"Mrs. Wexham?"

"Yes?"

"You owe me —"

"I owe you!" she exclaimed. "I've got it. Beasely is the plumber, Cooper is the tree man. You just have to be the bush boy, and I must owe you at least a thousand dollars, right? Big bucks, big bucks!"

The kid shook his head wildly, then offered her a weak grin. "Lady, I'm just the chicken-delivery boy, and your kids ordered a family bucket. You only owe me ten ninety-nine. And a tip is usually nice, but . . ."

His voice trailed away.

Becky winced inwardly. 'Twas the season!

"I'm sorry," she murmured. "Really sorry. As long as it's under a thousand, you can get your tip."

She swung back to Beasely and Cooper. "Will you excuse me, gentlemen?" Leeches! she thought. "I'll just pay for the chicken. I can afford *it*. I'll be back with you both in a minute."

"Sure thing, Mrs. Wexham," Beasely told her cheerfully.

But when she turned around to head back for her car and her purse, the chicken-delivery boy was gone. There was a new car in her driveway.

For a moment she paused in confusion. Then she recognized the car and the sandy-haired man leaning against it.

Tim. Yeagher.

She knew his silver-gray BMW right away. It wasn't really a new car, not a flashy one. It was a few years old, and he took good care of it. Those times when they had gone out, she'd noticed the difference in their cars. His was meticulously cared for.

Hers was usually in need of a cleaning.

There were fast-food Coke cups smashed on the floor. Schoolbooks strewn here and there, library books to be returned, some piece of costume left over from her last job, maybe even a french fry or two on the floor.

It had just gone to show her, she'd never really had a chance.

She'd been careful to keep him away from her home just because so many mornings did go like this one was going. But it hadn't really mattered. She'd managed to start a relationship with him without even bringing him home.

At least the kids had never known about her almost-involvement with him.

He was wearing sunglasses, so she couldn't really read his expression. But he leaned back comfortably against the car, as if he had been there for some time.

Long enough to see her talk to Beasely and Cooper.

And jump down the poor delivery boy's throat.

She stared at him blankly.

He smiled. A slow little half smile. Well, sure. He had to be amused.

"Got a minute?" he asked politely.

"If I can find a misplaced delivery boy, yes," she said.

Tim Yeagher shook his head. "The chicken

is on the porch. I paid the kid."

"*You* paid him!" she said in dismay. "But —"

"I promised him he'd get a much better tip from me, and he seemed to believe it right away."

"I don't need you to pay for my chicken!"

Tim waved a hand in the air impatiently. "It was ten ninety-nine, Becky!"

"That's not the point!"

"Becky, the chicken doesn't matter. Make dinner for me sometime. Buy me lunch. It isn't a big deal, okay?"

It *was* a big deal. She felt ridiculously close to crying. She hated him to see her in difficulty, and she certainly didn't want to appear to be some kind of charity case!

"It's chicken, for God's sake!" Tim insisted.

Relent! she warned herself. She nodded stiffly. It was the best she could manage. "Thanks, then." She cleared her throat. "So what — are you doing here?"

"I came to talk to you about Davey."

Her heart took another little slam against her throat. "Yes?"

"Well, you told me how important the team is to him. And I'd like to help, Becky. I really would. He's a good kid, and I understand that maybe he needs the team a little more than some of the others. But as I told you, I don't choose alone. So he's got to pick up on his batting a little."

"He did hit the ball yesterday," Becky said stubbornly.

Tim nodded. "He hit it. But this is Little League. Most of the coaches know the players. He's weak, and he's got to come out there slugging away."

Becky stared at him blankly again. He was speaking so seriously now. She tried to keep her eyes directly on his, but she was tempted to let them fall. He was such a good-looking man. In the nicest way. He wasn't overly muscular, but he was tall and nicely built. His sandy hair was all there, and he had a habit of shoving back a little lock that fell over his left eye. His features were nice masculine features.

He wore his jeans and T-shirt nicely.

His BVDs were well tucked into his pants.

She remembered the first time that they had met, literally crashing into each other at the television station where he worked, when she had been interviewed on the local *Working Women* show. His papers had flown all over, and she had stooped down to help him pick them up and nearly knocked him over. They'd wound up laughing, and they'd gone to lunch, and it had been the first time in her memory since Steven had died that she'd had fun with a man, that she'd laughed, that she'd felt at all desirable and as if there might be . . .

Something more. Something left.

They'd started going out, and things had only gotten better. But then she'd had to start canceling dates. Justin's fender-bender, Davey's cold, Paige's desperate all-night studying for a test, Justin's basketball tryouts. Tim Yeagher had never been married. His world was as orderly as his car. She'd tried to shelter him from the chaos of her own life, and she'd tried to hide it when she'd realized that she'd be seeing him at the Little League field. But then everything had exploded in the huge argument that night, and that had been it.

She had realized that all that was left for her in the world were strange little men with beady eyes and underwear that popped out over their beltlines.

Well, that was all in the past now. Odd that he was standing in her driveway now, a flicker of amusement still in his eyes from her encounter with the chicken-delivery boy. She gave herself a mental shake. Davey was at stake here. He had come to talk to her about Davey.

"There's only one thing he wants in the whole world," she said softly. "Just one thing that he wants for Christmas. To be on that all-star team. Well, he wants a signed Babe

Ruth card, too, and Justin wants a Porsche and he knows he's not getting it, either. Davey just really wants that team. And he's so coachable! He's the nicest kid —"

"Becky!" he said softly. "You don't have to convince me. Davey's a great kid. You're not listening. He's just got to bat better."

Becky stared at him. She set her hands on her hips, shaking her head. "If you came over here just to make my weekend miserable, the plumber is way ahead of you."

He smiled. "I came over to tell you that I've got some free time this afternoon. Send Davey over to the park, and I'll do my best to give him a couple hours of batting practice."

"What?" Becky breathed.

"I'm going to try to give him a few pointers. Maybe I can help. I don't know. But it's worth a try."

His words began to sink in. He was going to take a special interest. He was going to do everything for Davey that he could.

"Is that all right?"

She couldn't speak at first. She nodded slowly, then more firmly.

"Yes. Yes." It took a great deal of effort. She had to swallow fiercely. "Thanks. Thank you."

He lifted both hands. "Hey. It's all that he wants for Christmas, right?"

She nodded. Her throat felt very tight.

"That, and a signed Babe Ruth baseball card," she managed to say at last.

"Fresh out of those," he told her. "Though I wouldn't mind having one myself. He'll have to ask Santa about the card."

"Umm," she murmured.

They were still just staring at each other.

"And what do you want for Christmas this year?" he asked her.

She smiled. "That's easy. A new septic tank."

"What a romantic!"

"I try," Becky said. She could feel the sun on her face. And suddenly, she could remember how easy it had been to be with him, how nice it had felt to have his arm around her shoulders. She'd almost felt young.

And she'd almost remembered what it was like . . .

To be in love.

All that was very elusive. Her need for a septic tank was real. Davey was real.

But she still found herself smiling at Tim. Maybe it was the Christmas season. Even with nasty fat men leaning on their horns in parking lots and the Beaselys and Coopers of the world rubbing their hands together and adding up their profit margins.

"So what do you want for Christmas?" she

asked in return. "I'd think that you have almost everything."

He shrugged. She felt like kicking herself. She'd almost forgotten that he'd stopped playing pro ball because a car accident had nearly cost him his leg.

But he smiled and answered politely. "I'm kind of like Davey, maybe. I don't think that there is a 'thing' I want really badly." He grinned. "Mom will send me new underwear. Lots of shirts. But what I really want . . ."

"Is?"

"I don't know. It isn't a thing," he told her. They were still staring at each other. Then he shrugged and pushed his body up from the car. He pointed to the porch. "Your chicken is getting cold."

"Oh!"

"Send Davey to the park about three, okay? Tell him I'll try real hard to be on time, and I won't be later than three-thirty."

"Thanks again!"

"Sure!"

He stepped into the car behind the wheel. Becky stared after him.

"Mrs. Wexham —"

It was Beasely again. That darned Beasely!

She spun around. "Work out some terms for me, will you? Stop with the 'big bucks' and make it workable! And excuse me, my chicken is getting cold!"

She then ignored Beasely and Cooper and hurried to the house, scooping up the bucket of chicken, not even noticing how badly the porch and the gingerbreading needed painting. She hurried into the entry. "Davey! Davey!"

Her nephew came running anxiously down the stairway. "You've got to be at the park today around three, okay? Coach Yeagher is going to give you some batting pointers."

Davey stared at her, his eyes widening. "Really?"

"Really!"

He grinned broadly. "Wow!"

She smiled. "Grab your cousins and bring the groceries in from the car, will you? We've got lots of popcorn to pop and string."

Davey spun around to do as he had been told.

Becky walked purposefully into the parlor, flicked on the stereo, and found a Christmas album.

Bing Crosby was singing "White Christmas." Davey stepped into the room, a bag of groceries in his arms.

"Aunt Becky?"

"Yes?"

"I'm really sorry about the septic tank going bad and all. It might have lasted longer if you hadn't had quite so many people in the house."

"Oh, Davey!" she exclaimed. "That's not true at all! The system is over sixty years old. It's just shot!" She gave him a fierce hug. "Big bucks" shot. She felt just a little bit hysterical, but she pulled away from Davey, grinning.

"Hey, it's all right!" she said. "Like the T-shirts say, 'Shit Happens'!"

Davey's eyes widened.

"Oh, God, I didn't say that!" Becky groaned.

But Davey was laughing. "It's okay, Aunt Becky. You should hear some of the guys at the park," he told her reassuringly. He ran on out of the parlor, and Becky sank into the old sofa, trying to decide why she suddenly felt just a little bit lighter when she still should have been depressed as all hell!

Chapter 3

The park was empty when Davey arrived that afternoon. It seemed strange. Usually, there were so many people about. The place was alive with shouts and sounds, kids playing, grown-ups talking. There was that great sound when a bat really connected hard with a ball, and it went sailing way out across a field and sometimes right over a fence.

Davey had never had that happen to him. But it could. Sometime. Coach Mac, who worked with Coach Yeagher a lot, had told him plenty of times that once he learned to really connect, he could make it sail, too. Coach Mac was fun. He liked to promise the kids a dollar if they could hit the ball, and then he'd pretend he was out of dollars, but he always had them again when the ice cream truck rolled around and every little kid on the field could line up with him and walk away with an ice cream.

Well, he would have to make the team to get to work with Coach Mac, too.

He left his glove and ball in the batter's

cage and walked up to the plate with his bat. He shuffled his feet and looked at his stance, staring down at the orange dust that arose, covering his cleats. Then he closed his eyes and tried to think of everything that the coaches had taught him. *Level swing, Davey. Watch the bat, watch the ball. Make it a level swing! Choke up, choke up, now! Watch the ball, let it get to you! Bend your knees. . . .*

He swung. A good, level swing. If there had been a ball coming his way, could he have connected with it?

Again. He concentrated. He swung his bat strongly. Whack! He could almost hear it! His bat would have connected with that ball, he was certain.

"Well, now, that was nice enough!" he heard suddenly.

Startled, Davey swung around.

There was a man watching him. A big man. At least six feet tall, maybe a little more. And solid. A big, big guy. That was all that Davey could see at first, because the sun was right behind the man and Davey had to squint hard to see at all. The sun was gold. Bright, dazzling. Davey kept blinking. The shadow of a man remained, with the emblazoning sun all around him.

Then the man stepped closer. Davey's eyes

widened. Yeah, the guy was big all right! And he was wearing an old uniform, an old *Yankee* uniform. He had fleshy cheeks and warm, sparkling little eyes in a somewhat jowly face.

Davey had seen that face before. Seen it thousands of times. He'd seen it every single time he had looked at his posters and magazines. That face belonged to the Babe.

He blinked. He might be a kid, but he wasn't dumb. The Babe was dead, he had died years and years ago. No matter how much Davey wanted him to be there, he couldn't possibly be. This just had to be someone else. Someone who looked a whole heck of a lot like the Babe.

Davey moistened his lips, realizing that he had been staring dumbly at the guy for a long time.

"You're never going to hit a ball, kid, just standing there with your jaw hanging slack."

Davey immediately closed his mouth. He heard his jaw snap. He was being pretty rude to whoever this guy was. He moistened his lips because they were just bone dry. "Hi," he managed to say.

The man walked toward him and reached for his bat. The guy was real, Davey determined. Flesh and blood.

And darn, but he sure did look just the spitting image of the Babe. George Herman Ruth. And Davey knew, because he had spent so much time looking at him, at his face, at the way he had stood in his pictures, posing with a bat.

"This is a good bat. A real good bat," the man said.

Davey was still staring. He swallowed hard. "My dad bought it for me."

"Before he died, huh?"

"How do you know he's dead?"

The man didn't answer. He had Davey's bat in his hands. Of course, the bat was really way too small for the big man, but he gave it a swing. It moved so fast, it was almost invisible. Davey blinked and stared at him again. Okay, he'd already been real rude, but if the man wanted to dress up like Babe Ruth, he had to expect people to stare at him.

"Who are you?" Davey demanded.

Those eyes, sparkling and warm, touched down on his. "What do you mean, who am I? You don't know who I am?"

"You sure do look like Babe Ruth."

"Well, then?"

Davey shook his head. He didn't know quite how to break it to the guy.

"Babe Ruth is . . . dead," he said at last. There was no nice way to put it.

The man smiled. He whizzed the bat

through the air after an imaginary ball once again.

"Yeah, I guess I am," he said reflectively.

Davey just stared. He didn't know where to go from here. He shuffled his feet, then studied the man again. He was the spitting image.

"Look," the big man said, pausing. "We don't have all that much time. Don't you think we ought to get started?"

"Get started?" Davey said blankly.

The man smiled again. It was a great smile. "If I've got this right, there was some little kid sitting on a bed last night holding one of my old caps. 'Just once,' Davey, that's what you said. If I could help you out just once, you know that you could learn to bat. Right?"

Davey's jaw fell again. He tried to think really logically. Maybe one of his cousins had heard him. Maybe this was a setup to make him look like a real little butthead.

No. They might fight now and then, he decided, but none of his cousins was that cruel.

"How many times have I gotta tell ya, kid?" the man asked him. "You can't bat with your jaw flapping around like that."

Davey closed his mouth. "You can't really be the Babe!"

"Why not?"

"Because . . ."

"Look, kid, you asked for me, and I'm here. And we haven't got all that much time before that Mr. Yeagher comes around, so we've got to get some hard work in. You ready?"

Davey tried to nod. "But why —"

"I got a thing for orphans. Mind you, I wasn't an orphan, like so many people seemed to think. My dad got to see me start to make the big time, though my mother had been gone a long time by then," he said softly. "It wasn't even that I was such a bad kid. It was just that times were tough, and if I wanted something, well, I thought I should just take it. My dad took me to St. Mary's because he had to. And it turned out just fine. St. Mary's was a good place. You know why?"

Davey just stared. He knew the story. But he liked hearing it again.

"I met Brother Matthias there. And he was the one to really get me started with baseball. He was the greatest man I ever knew. He saw some talent in me right away." The bat was leveled at Davey. "Other people might be proud of having gone to Harvard. I was every bit as proud to have gone to St. Mary's. Don't you forget that, kid."

Davey smiled. "I know. I read lots of biographies on you."

The man swung the bat. "So you know now that I'm the Babe, huh?"

Davey blinked. Did he?

Of course not! Babe Ruth was dead!

But then again . . .

"You held the cap, kid. And you wished for me."

"But how?"

The big man shrugged. "Think of me as an early Christmas present from someone who really cares. How's that?"

Did it matter? This guy really knew how to swing a bat, and he sure knew how to act like Babe Ruth!

"Can you help me?" Davey asked.

"You're a worker, kid. But that's what's needed. Know what Brother Matthias used to do, and what he got me into doing? He'd take his left hand and throw up the ball, and smack it with the bat. Sometimes he'd clear fences that way. Over and over. Sometimes he'd do it for hours. Now, that isn't like having a pitcher come at you with a fast ball, but it's darn good practice. The eye to the ball and all that. I had talent, but I still had to work hard. It was a little different for me, 'cause I'm a —"

"Lefty," Davey supplied.

"Yeah. But I had to work, you've got to work. Hard."

Davey nodded.

The Babe — even if he wasn't the Babe,

Davey decided he was still going to pretend that he was for the moment — gave him another smile. It was such a great smile. The smile from a man who really liked kids, who really cared about them.

"Let's get started. Okay, first things first. I noticed when I came up that you're not stepping into the ball. You gotta step into it, it's all one motion. I'm going to pitch to you. Did you know that I started off as a pitcher?"

Davey grinned and nodded.

"Yeah, yeah, of course, you knew." Out on the pitcher's mound now, George Herman Ruth smiled. Davey grinned from ear to ear. The Babe was about to pitch to him.

And he did. Easy pitches — the Babe was so good that he could *let* Davey hit every one of them when he chose. He called out instructions, and Davey bit down hard on his lip and did his best to follow them. Then the Babe came and stood behind Davey and held the bat with him and helped him step into an imaginary pitch. Davey listened avidly and tried his hardest.

"You're gettin' it, kid. I swear, you're getting it! Now, if you can just learn to relax with all you've learned, well, then, you just might be okay."

Davey stared at the man again. He had to

be the Babe. The real Babe. With those sparkling, dark, soulful eyes, with his quick smile. The way he talked, the way he moved. But how could it be?

Don't question it! he told himself. Don't question it! He's just a Christmas present from someone who cares.

Davey was willing to leave it at that.

They were finished. The big man walked back toward him again, smiling broadly. He ruffled Davey's hair. "I always was a sucker for an orphan! But you're not in such bad shape, huh, kid?"

Davey shrugged. His gaze lowered. "Aunt Becky's the greatest. It's just that I'm — I'm a hardship."

The Babe shook his head. "She loves you, kid. You're no hardship. You're a great kid — you just remember that. And it doesn't matter if you can play ball or not, you got that?"

Davey started to nod.

"Hey, Davey!"

Someone was calling his name. He turned around to look. Out past the fence, Tim Yeagher had just pulled into the parking lot.

"There's Tim —" Davey started to say, turning back. But no one was there. He was staring into the sun again, and it was strong and dazzling, and it stung his eyes. But there was no big shadow there. No big man.

No Babe.

He was gone. Just as if he had never been.

But he had been there! He had been. And he had worked hard with Davey.

"Davey! Did you hear me?" Tim was walking up, a duffel bag of equipment over his shoulder, his limp just slightly noticeable. A younger man than George Herman Ruth, thinner. But there was something in Tim that reminded Davey of the Babe.

"Did you hear me? I'm really sorry I'm so late. I was running behind to begin with, and I got a flat out by my place and had to change it. You been here long?"

Davey shook his head. "It's okay, coach. I — I'm just really grateful that you're going to help me."

Tim grinned and knelt down to tie a sneaker that had come undone. It was a nice grin. Davey knew why Tim had reminded him of the Babe. "You like kids, don't you, Coach Yeagher?" Davey asked.

Yeagher looked up curiously. He shrugged and grinned again. "What's not to like?" He stood, ruffling Davey's hair. "Let's get started."

To Davey's sinking disappointment, it was an awful afternoon. He remembered everything that the Babe had said to him, and he concentrated on everything that Tim Yeagher was saying, too. But something was wrong. Maybe he was just still unnerved by what had happened. Had the Babe really been there? Or had Davey just gone kind of crazy and imagined the whole thing?

And if Babe Ruth had been there, would he come back? No, Davey reasoned. When he had held the cap, he had wished that the Babe could help him just one time. The Babe had given him that one time.

"Choke it, choke it!" Tim cried to him from the pitcher's mound.

But the ball sailed past him.

Finally, Tim came walking up to him, set an arm on his shoulder, and led him back to the cage where they had left the rest of the equipment. "We'll work again," he promised.

"I stunk, huh?" Davey said.

"You weren't concentrating. And I know how badly you want this, so I think that maybe we just need to start over fresh. What do you think?"

Davey nodded, swallowing. He was making a worse and worse impression every time. "Thanks. Thanks, really. I appreciate it a whole lot."

"I know, Davey. And that's why it's worth all my time."

Davey tried to smile. Then his mouth felt

a little dry, and he decided that he might take a stab at getting Tim and Aunt Becky together right now.

"Want to come to dinner?" Davey said. He said it really quickly. Too quickly. It probably sounded fishy.

"Dinner?"

Davey nodded strenuously. "Dinner. My aunt Becky is a great cook, and she's so glad that you're helping me, I know that she'd be happy to have you. Please come."

Tim looked at him and shook his head. "I really don't think so."

"Oh, yeah. You've probably got a date or something, right?"

"What is this? The third degree?" Tim asked, laughing. He hiked his equipment bag over his shoulder. "I'm covered with baseball dust —"

"Aunt Becky loves baseball dust. Honest."

Davey watched Tim hesitate again. Amazing, but it seemed that he almost had him. "Please?" he repeated.

And Tim Yeagher relented. "You're sure she won't mind?"

"She'll be happy, honest! I know she won't mind a bit!"

Would she? Davey wondered. He kept his smile glued in place. Aunt Becky was going to mind, but that was only because she didn't really know what was good for her yet.

"Yep, thrilled!" Davey said. He kept on grinning, but he winced inside.

"Come on. Hop on in the car then, Davey."

He did as he was told. And stared straight ahead.

He'd never — never! — even in his wildest dreams imagined that he might have gotten Tim Yeagher to come home with him today.

Why, that was almost as amazing as the fact that Babe Ruth had appeared on the baseball field to help him!

No matter what she did this Christmas season, Becky decided mournfully, it didn't seem to work out. She, Paige, Justin, and Jacob had gone out for a tree. She'd seen the most beautiful Douglas fir, and she'd even managed to wrangle a great deal on its price — an unusual accomplishment for her these days.

But even in the tree lot, she had to admit, Justin had warned her about its size. "That's a big tree, Mom."

"We've got a big house."

"Not that big."

"We'll trim it down."

And they had trimmed it. Trimmed it and trimmed it, and now, it looked much more like a giant green pear than a Christmas tree.

Limbs and fallen needles were everywhere in the entry, in the hall, in the parlor. They'd spent hours with the lights, but half of them weren't working, and the light boxes were strewn everywhere. She couldn't find the extension cord. Jacob had dropped a box of ornaments, but he was saying that it was all Justin's fault, that his brother had tripped him.

Then the doorbell rang.

"I'll get it, I'll get it!" Paige cried.

Her daughter ran to the door. Becky stood up, suddenly convinced that on top of everything else, she was burning something in the kitchen.

"Hey, it was your fault, *idiot!*" Justin raged at Jacob.

"Your fault, *dimwit!*" Justin started back. But he broke off. He was staring at the doorway to the parlor.

Davey was home. And not alone. He had brought Tim Yeagher with him.

Becky was staring at the doorway, too. So once again, there was Tim, striking, poised bachelor, watching her in the midst of complete domestic chaos!

Worse. Her hair was in tangles around her face, she didn't have on a stitch of makeup, and she had Christmas tree sap stains on her worn tailored blouse.

Oh, hell. She just couldn't win. She didn't think she'd ever felt quite so hysterical in all her life.

She forced herself to smile. "Hello. Welcome to my home, Mr. Yeagher." She was going to laugh or cry any second. "Please, allow me to introduce you around. There's my son Idiot, as you just heard his brother, Dimwit, address him. Then there's my daughter — they like to call her Numbnutts, and since you've just brought home the one they like to call Butthead, I guess we're all here!"

"Mother!" Paige gasped.

Jacob didn't seem to be having any problems with the situation. About two years older than Davey — but always confident and maybe just a bit too reckless — he walked up to Tim, his hands on his hips. Then he extended one hand. "Hi. I'm Dimwit. Welcome to the zoo. I've seen you around the park, Mr. Yeagher. All the kids say that you're just great. I hope you'll still stay to dinner, even if you have to eat with some people with real weird names."

Tim grinned and took Jacob's hand. Becky suddenly wanted to slap the lot of them and send them all to bed without any supper — including Tim Yeagher.

"I think I know you all," Tim said, smiling

from one child to the next. "Paige, Justin, and Jacob." He set his hands on Davey's shoulders and drew him forward. "And Butthead, of course."

Becky tightened her jaw, watching Tim. He was such a natural with the kids. She even resented him for a moment. He stood there so easily with his great car outside and his handsome face and his almost perfect physique. Maybe it was easy for him to be relaxed. He had just brought Davey home. He could go back out to his great car and drive back to the peace and quiet and sanity of his own place and maybe feel as if he had done his good deed for the day, dining with them all.

And his septic system was probably working just fine.

But as her eyes touched his, he smiled and shrugged. It was a great smile. She felt just a little bit ashamed. Tim Yeagher had managed to roll with a bunch of punches. Maybe she was determined to judge him harshly.

Just so that she could convince herself that she wasn't really missing something wonderful by missing him.

"Becky, if dinner is a problem, I really don't need to stay. Davey —"

"You're more than welcome to dinner," Becky said quickly. She wanted Davey to know that it was his home, that he could invite people into it.

"You're definitely welcome to *my* dinner!" Jacob assured him. "Meat loaf. Ugh!" He wrinkled his nose.

Meat loaf! It was already burning. "Excuse me!" Becky suddenly exclaimed. She leaped over the piles of boxes and went jostling past Jacob, Davey, and Tim, desperate to reach the kitchen. She skidded to the oven in record speed, but it didn't matter, it was too late. Way too late.

Clouds of gray steam and smoke filled the kitchen as she opened the door. She grabbed the sheep-face potholders Justin had bought for her birthday three years ago and pulled out the pan, throwing it on top of the stove. Dismayed, she coughed, choked, and waved the gray mist away from it.

She turned around. Tim was leaning in the kitchen doorway. He was still smiling.

"Would you quit that?" she demanded.

"Quit what?"

"Quit smiling like that."

"Oh," he said, and nodded gravely. "Got a beer?"

She nodded strenuously. "In the refrigerator. Help yourself. Burnt meat loaf goes much better with beer. A lot of it."

He helped himself to a beer. "I think I'll

go see if I can do anything with the lights," he told her. But he didn't leave right away. He kind of looked her up and down, and then he was grinning again. "It's a definite look," he said.

"You don't have to stay, you know," she hissed.

"I wouldn't miss this for the world."

He walked away and Becky stared after him. Then she tried to remember what she had been doing. Was there any way to salvage this thing?

No — dump it all and send out for pizza.

But she really couldn't afford to dump a meal, not with Christmas — and the septic tank.

She stared at her meat loaf, frowning. Then she plucked it from the pan to a plate and did her best to repair it.

Actually, all in all, it wasn't half as bad as she had thought it would be — not that even *half-bad* was really *good.* But Paige came wandering in to help her and set the table really beautifully. Becky trimmed away most of the scorched top of the meat loaf and made a decent gravy to ladle over it, and it wound up looking pretty good.

She'd bought good Idaho potatoes and it was almost impossible to wreck them, so they were served along with lots of butter and sour cream and chives. She made a Caesar salad, and at the last minute she found one of the bottles of red wine she had bought with the kids at the Biltmore estate in Asheville, North Carolina, on spring break.

When she came out to the parlor to call everyone, the Christmas lights were working. Tim was stretched out on the floor, having just connected the last string. Davey, Jacob, and Justin were all on their knees or hunkered down by him, and they were enthusiastically discussing baseball heroes.

"Dinner," she said softly.

"Oh, boy, meat loaf!" Jacob cried.

She gave her son a look of cast daggers. He smiled innocently. At his side, even Davey grinned.

"Jacob, one more word, and you'll be in bed," she said warningly.

"Promise?" he asked her hopefully.

"Get to the table, kid!" Tim told him.

Jacob and Davey grinned and shot on by. Tim looked at Becky. "Meat loaf. Oh, boy," he said.

She swung around and started for the table herself.

They all started passing plates around and eating, then Justin elbowed Jacob and Jacob started to howl. "Grace! We're supposed to be saying grace. We always say grace, Mr. Yeagher."

"What?" Jacob said.

"Davey, you go ahead," Paige said sweetly.

Becky was ready to crash her head against the table.

"All join hands!" Paige suggested cheerfully. They did, Tim at one end, Becky at the other. Justin and Paige on one side, Jacob and Davey on the other.

Davey muttered out a grace faster than Becky had ever heard words spoken.

"Let's eat!" Justin said.

"Oh, boy, meat loaf!" Paige said sweetly, offering Tim one of her beautiful smiles.

"Have some wine," Becky advised.

He was still smiling, damn him! Rolling with the punches. He opened the wine expertly, came and poured her a glass, then walked back around and poured his own while the food was being passed around the table.

Thank God, the wine was good.

And so was Tim. He seemed to eat without any problems, and he was easy with the kids. Hands and arms stretched in front of him, and he didn't seem to mind.

He bit into the meat loaf. "It's good!" he told Becky.

"See!" Davey swung on her. "It's good!" he cried. Of course, he swung so fast that the potato he'd just set his fork into went flying.

It landed right in Tim's plate. In his gravy. And the gravy bounced up onto the old baseball shirt he was wearing.

"Oh!" Becky leaped up. She dunked her napkin into her water and went rushing down to the other end of the table. She knelt down beside him, rubbing away at the gravy. Then she felt his fingers closing around her wrist, and she looked up into his eyes. "It's all right!" he said.

She was suddenly very aware that she was kneeling beside him, that he was so close that she could feel his warmth and breath in the fading scent of his aftershave. Her fingers were skimming over his bare flesh as she held his shirt to scrub away at it.

A blush flooded her cheeks.

Why? They'd been this close before. But she'd called it off — she'd had to!

She stood quickly. "Sorry!"

"Becky, the shirt is a wreck. I've been playing baseball in it all day."

She nodded. She walked back around to her seat. She tried to smile and nod and make the kids feel that she was behaving normally, that Tim was just a casual friend, *Davey's* guest.

And Tim, damn him, continued to be just wonderful. He laughed, he talked, he ate.

But he'd go home. And tomorrow night,

he just might have a date with the attractive brunette anchor at the television station. They'd be dressed up, and they'd go to a nice restaurant, and they'd sip drinks and eat — without wearing the food — and he'd laugh and tell her about the wild house where he'd had dinner with some of the kids from the baseball field.

Unfair! And wrong, she told herself. It was hard sometimes, yes. But she loved the kids. She wouldn't trade her world for anyone else's.

But then again, she wouldn't expect anyone else to love her world the way she did.

He left soon after dinner. The lights were working, they'd made the popcorn strings and strung them, the kitchen had been cleaned up. Tim managed to get Becky to walk him to the door.

"Thanks. It was really great."

She shook her head. "You don't have to say that."

"Becky, honest, it was great. You're a magician, really. The meat loaf looked great — and tasted great. It was all great."

"Right. Wearing gravy was great."

He grinned. She gritted her teeth. Enough! Fine. Be gracious. Say thanks. She really loved the warmth of his smile. It was what had attracted her to him in the first place.

"Becky, I didn't mind wearing the gravy at all. Because it was sure great having you try to clean it off my shirt!"

She arched a brow at him, then felt his hands on her shoulders. He pulled her close and kissed her on the forehead. "See you, Becky," he murmured.

He had probably been gone awhile before she felt the cool evening breeze and realized that she was standing there, looking after his car — which had long since disappeared. She closed the door and wandered back into the parlor.

The Christmas tree lights were twinkling away. The kids were miraculously subdued, just watching the lights.

"Umm. Bedtime, guys," she murmured.

Not even Jacob argued. They all kissed her and wandered upstairs. Davey paused for just a minute. "It was all right to invite him, wasn't it, Aunt Becky?"

She nodded. "It was all right to invite him."

"I think he *likes* you."

"Of course he likes me. He's a nice man. He likes people."

"No, I think he *likes* you."

"Davey, I'm not sure how to make you understand this, but that would be a miracle."

His eyes brightened. He smiled at her

broadly. "Aunt Becky, miracles do happen!"

She had to smile. He was so determined. "Sure they do," she told him. She gave him a tight hug. "Go on to bed now. It's not easy dragging you all out of bed in the morning!"

Davey, still smiling away, left the parlor, skipping toward the stairs. She shook her head after him, bewildered, but delighted to see him so happy.

She watched the lights for a while. Miracles did happen. Tim had made the lights work.

She leaned back. If only he could make other things work, too. . . .

She pulled the pillow from the couch. It would be so nice if he really could care for her, and if it didn't matter that she came with an instant family and a decaying house and a shot septic tank.

The little things just seemed . . . so damned nice. Having him at dinner. Maybe sitting on this sofa, curled up together. Resting her head on his shoulder. He had a great shoulder. Like his smile. Like his eyes.

"What would *I* like for Christmas?" she mused aloud, staring at the tree. "You."

She leaned her head down. Tears were stinging her eyes. Well, maybe a miracle was happening for Davey. She was so glad for him. She didn't have the right to expect another one.

She leaned her head down on the sofa and remembered that pleasant fading scent of aftershave, and suddenly, with nearly painful nostalgia, she was remembering their dates, remembering the incredible feel of his kiss. Holding his hand, *caring.*

The lights kept twinkling. *It would be nice. . . .*

Chapter 4

The park was exceptionally quiet late Sunday morning.

Davey was still partly dressed up when he walked over to it, shuffling his feet in the dirt, then realizing that he was covering his good shoes with orange baseball dust. Not that he was *that* dressed up. Aunt Becky had taken them all to church that morning. When Jacob complained, she assured them all that it was simply a punishment for Jacob, God had created all churches for just that reason. But she had told Davey once that it didn't matter what they grew up to be, what religion they chose, just so long as they understood something about what really mattered.

And what really mattered was being a good person, which meant being careful of other people's lives and feelings. She didn't make them dress up — this was Florida, and people were a little bit casual here. So he wore his good shoes and his good jeans and a striped shirt. He must have looked funny now, in the middle of a baseball field.

"What, no baseball bat?"

He swung around. The Babe was back. Davey's eyes widened and he blinked, but the Babe was still there. Tall, big, dominating the scene. He was in his Sunday clothes, too, white shirt, blue tie, black trousers, and jacket. But he was still wearing a baseball cap, he still had the look of a jowly cheeked hound, and he still had his great dark, twinkling eyes. He had to be a ghost, or maybe just imagination. It didn't matter. Davey didn't really want to question why he was there. He just was.

Davey smiled and shrugged. "We just got back from church. I came out for a walk, that's all." He paused. "How can you be here? When I was wishing on your baseball cap that you could help me, I said once. Just once."

"Want me to go away?" the Babe asked.

"Never!"

The Babe wandered over to sit down on the second rung of the bleachers facing field three. Davey hurried along to sit next to him. "I'm really grateful," Davey assured him worriedly.

The Babe tousled his hair. "You wished for just once. Sometimes you wish for things and you can't have them. Then sometimes you get more than what you wished for. How's that?"

"That's great."

"So how did you do the other day?"

"Awful," Davey admitted with a weary sigh. "Just awful."

"Hmm." The Babe thought on that for a minute. "Well, we'll just keep working." He studied Davey with a puzzled expression. "Awful?"

"I think I was maybe just a little bit nervous. On account of the way that you sort of appeared and disappeared."

"Oh. Well, you'll be used to that kind of thing from now on."

Davey grinned. "Yeah."

"Well, you need to run home and get changed and get your stuff. I'll pitch you some balls. I did tell you I started out as a pitcher, right, kid?"

Davey nodded.

"Got there by kind of being a wise guy. I was giving some buddies of mine a hard time in a game once, and Brother Matthias dragged me out. He told me that if I thought I could do a better job, I'd better start doing it. Surprised the heck out of both of us when I could pitch. That's just it, Davey. You don't know if you can do it until you try. And try real hard."

Davey jumped up. "I'm going to get my stuff, okay? I'll be right back. You won't go away?"

"I won't go away."

Davey started to run toward the house, but then he paused and looked back. "You really are a great man, Mr. Ruth. A great, great man."

The Babe stood up and studied Davey. "Thanks, kid. I caused my share of problems."

Davey shrugged. "Yeah, well . . ."

"But I always did like kids. Kids are great, Davey. You remember that. Now hurry."

Davey hurried. Aunt Becky was already gone on an afternoon job at the mall, Paige was studying, and Jacob and Justin were fighting over the Nintendo.

He changed quickly and grabbed his stuff, racing back to the park. His heart was pounding. He had to be crazy to think he was seeing the Babe, right? If the Babe had disappeared, then maybe Davey wasn't quite so crazy.

But the Babe hadn't disappeared. If he was a ghost, or pure imagination, he still looked darned good. When Davey arrived back at the park, he was just sitting on the bench, waiting, watching the field as if a game were taking place there.

"You're back." The Babe stood up and took off his jacket and rolled up his sleeves. "Let's get to work."

* * *

For Sunday afternoon Becky had taken a job at the mall as Santa Claus. She was a little small for the role, but then as Christmas came closer and closer, the malls couldn't afford to be quite so picky. Being Santa was all right. Her knees were bruised, and her chin chafed from the beard, and a few precious little tykes had told her that Santa had an awful high voice. One of them asked what Santa wanted for Christmas. That was easy — kids that weighed less.

On Monday, when she played a tap-dancing reindeer once again, Becky began to think that the Santa role hadn't been so bad. The dancing was fun, it was a cute show, and she certainly knew it by rote, but it was tiring, too. She worried all afternoon, aware that Davey would be having another tryout for the team. She managed to catch him at the house between school and the tryout and wish him luck, and he seemed cheerful enough over the phone. That seemed like a good sign.

The mall would stay open till nine that night. She was offered a huge bonus if she would stay until it closed. She was tired and worried, and she wanted to say no, but she couldn't forget the septic tank and "big bucks, big bucks, Mrs. Wexham!"

She stayed.

It was nearly ten by the time she dragged her bone-weary body into the house. She was braced for anything, but for once, all seemed to be in good order. Paige had made a salad and called for pizza. Justin assured her that he had meticulously cleaned up all the paper plates. Hard work, but somebody had to do it. Davey seemed a little subdued, but he was still cheerful when he told her about the tryout. No, he hadn't been cut. Yet.

"Bed, guys," she told them. "You're up awfully late for children."

"We're hardly children, Mother," Paige told her with great dignity. "Justin and me, that is."

"Justin and *I*. All right, then, but Jacob and Davey —"

"Hey, I'm older than he is!" Jacob chimed in.

"You're still a kid," she told her son. A cute kid. He had his dad's endless confidence and easy manner. She wished that some of Jacob's manner would rub off on Davey, that he wouldn't worry so much, that he wouldn't want so much, that he wouldn't *hurt* so much. "Go to bed." They all looked at her. She started waving them toward the stairway. "Go to bed. Go directly to bed. Do not pass go, do not collect money, or whatever it is. Bed!"

They all laughed and obeyed her. She bit her lip. It hadn't been a bad night. She was ready to keel over and she'd worked all day, but the house was still standing and the kids hadn't killed each other.

Now, a shower.

The shower was bliss, but she needed more.

Her feet were killing her. She hadn't minded spending the day as a tap-dancing reindeer — really, the kids at the mall all enjoyed the Christmas shows so much — but now she was feeling the wear and tear of the overtime. She dragged the big bucket out from beneath the sink, loaded it liberally with Epsom salts and warm water, then sank her feet in, taking a chair at the kitchen table. It was almost heaven. The steam rose all around her.

Heaven? She must be getting old. It was certainly pathetic to realize that soaking her feet was almost heaven!

She closed her eyes and leaned back anyway. She had just gotten somewhat comfortable when she heard an insistent knock on the door.

"No," she moaned aloud. "Go away."

But the knocking didn't stop. It had to be about the septic tank or the trees, she thought. They wanted to start in the morning. They wanted money.

She patted her feet dry hastily and waddled

to the front door in an old pink terry robe, pushing her hair out of her face. She paused at the door, having lived alone long enough to learn to be careful and look through the peephole. Someone was looking back at her. She gasped and hopped away.

"Becky! Let me in. I've got to talk to you."

Her heart sank. Tim. Oh, great. He had been here for the Christmas tree and meat loaf fiasco, and now he was here for her frayed terry robe, no makeup, and bare feet. At least she didn't have cold cream on her face. But that was only because she didn't use it. If she did, he would have definitely come when she was wearing it.

She could ignore him.

"Becky, can I talk to you? It's about Davey."

She opened the door, staring at him. He must have been working late, too. He looked immaculate in a tan suit, a great tie, even a vest.

She folded her arms over her chest and backed away from the door.

"Yes?"

"Are you inviting me in?"

She stepped farther back. "Of course." Then she hesitated. "Would you like some coffee or something?"

"Yeah, maybe. No, I guess it's kind of

late, isn't it? Are the kids all in bed?"

She nodded, and he followed suit. For all his usual confidence, he seemed uncomfortable tonight.

"What is it?" she asked him.

Hands on his hips, he paced the entryway. Then he paused in front of her. "I just wanted to talk to you. Because I don't want you to be terribly disappointed."

"Davey didn't make the team after all."

He shook his head. "No, he did make the cuts today. He was batting a lot better."

"So I heard. That's wonderful," she said.

"So were some of the other kids. They were outstanding. But what I really want to say is this. Even if he doesn't make this team, Becky, I want to keep working with him. He's a great kid. He lacks some skill, but he's got the heart to make up for it. He's coachable. He watches for all the signs, and he runs like a little rabbit. I just want you to know that I'm going to keep working with him, no matter what."

Becky inhaled and exhaled. Tim was a nice man, a good man. Well, she had known that when she was first attracted to him. A long drink of water in a long thirsty desert . . .

But here he was tonight, trying to break disappointment to her as gently as possible.

And worse than that, she couldn't possibly

have looked more like a dried-out bag of bones.

She tried to smile. "You don't know what this team means to Davey," she said softly.

"I haven't given up. But don't get your heart set on it. Like I said, I want to keep working with Davey either way. And I'd like to start seeing his aunt again, too."

Becky arched a brow. No. No, she had tried this already. "It didn't work, Tim."

"Because you wouldn't let it," he said.

Her knees felt a little rubbery. She felt like Davey, wanting to make the team so badly. Oh, God, yes, she wanted to see him.

But she didn't want to suffer the kind of disappointment that would come when he tired of a thirtysomething widow with four dependents.

"I'm hell on men," she said.

"I beg your pardon?"

"They die on me," she said softly.

He grinned. "This is not *The Importance of Being Earnest*! Your husband died, Becky. It wasn't your fault."

"My brother died, too."

"And it wasn't carelessness on your part. Remember that from the play when it's implied that losing *two* family members is just that? Becky, your losses are *tragic*. They're *not* your fault. Dinner. Friday. I'm willing to take my chances."

"I don't —"

"It's just dinner!"

"All right! Dinner! Friday!"

"What time do I pick you up?"

She hesitated, trying to remember her schedule for the week. Paige wouldn't mind staying home with the younger boys, and Justin would have to act his age and do it, too. But work . . .

"Don't pick me up. How about I meet you at eight?"

"Maxine's?"

"Fine."

"Great. Great," he said. It was as if he hadn't really expected her to agree. Suddenly, he almost jumped out of the doorway.

"What — ?" she began.

"I'm leaving before you change your mind!" he said, and pulled the door shut himself. Becky leaned against it for a moment. She smiled.

She was a fool.

Ah, well, he *was* what she had wanted for Christmas! Even if it was just for one nice dinner at Maxine's.

Funny. Her feet didn't even hurt anymore.

She remembered Davey. She opened the door to the night and looked up at the stars.

"If there are miracles, God, let Davey have one, please!"

The stars twinkled back down at her. She watched the endlessly beautiful sky for a while, then closed the door and went up to bed herself.

She was grateful then for being a tap-dancing reindeer. Tap-dancing reindeer got so exhausted that they slept easily, no matter what was plaguing their hearts or minds.

Most of the time, his cousins were okay. Paige was really all right — she actually seemed to prefer Davey to both her brothers most of the time. She was older, though, and she could be very superior at times, but mostly, she was okay.

And Jacob was all right to be around most of the time, too. He called Davey butthead a lot, but like Jacob, Justin called everyone butthead.

Jacob was the toughest in the house, Davey thought, and he thought it often.

They were the closest in age. Jacob was only about two years older than he. He also had a natural athletic ability that was a pain in the — hind end. He liked to tease Davey, and maybe he even liked to remind him that he was the adopted one in the household, not quite as good.

The near disaster of that Tuesday had occurred because of Jacob.

Davey had come home from school, minding his own business. He'd been up in his own room — minding his own business once again — when Jacob had come in. Without knocking. He'd picked up Davey's baseball and started tossing it up into the air again and again. "You catch okay, you know that, Davey?" he told him.

"Yeah, I can usually catch okay," Davey said warily.

Jacob shook his head sadly. "You're never going to make these cuts. I think you're trying to make this team so that Tim Yeagher will have to hang around with Mom a little. That's not a bad idea. Heck, we could sure come up with someone a whole lot worse, right?"

"Yeah, right," Davey agreed, still cautious.

His cousin grinned, then shook his head sadly. "Good idea. kid. But it isn't going to work. You can't learn to bat in time."

"I *am* going to learn to bat in time," Davey said defensively.

"You'd need a miracle."

"I'm getting a miracle," he told his cousin, the words rushing from him too quickly. "I've got real help. The Babe is helping me."

"*What?*" Jacob said incredulously.

Too late, Davey realized his mistake. He had to be careful, really careful.

"I'm reading —" he began, but Jacob was already hooting with laughter. *"The Babe? The Babe?"* he exclaimed. He was laughing so hard, he fell on Davey's bed. "The great Babe Ruth comes swooping down from heaven — or from wherever he went! — to help my butthead cousin learn to bat!" He wagged a finger at Davey. "Ah, yes! I can see it now! Babe Ruth, visiting at our front door! I can't wait to tell Justin. And Paige. Davey sees ghosts! Hey, maybe you can get our folks back down here, too. Your mom and both our dads!"

Maybe Jacob was a little bit upset then, too, but he'd done it to himself.

"Stop it!" Davey was shouting and imploring, but Jacob was already up, racing out of the room. "Hey, guys! The butthead talks to ghosts! Babe Ruth is here! He's coming to dinner. Get this — he's going to teach Davey how to bat!"

"What?" Davey heard Justin say from downstairs. Then there was murmuring, and laughter. Then he heard Paige laughing, too.

He raced to the doorway, blood coloring his face, and shouted down, "At least I care! At least I want something good for Aunt Becky. She's your mother! Maybe you think you don't have to care, maybe you don't know what it's like to lose both parents." He hesitated a minute. He wasn't accustomed to using the language that came to some kids so easily. "You just go to hell! All of you — you just go to hell!"

He slammed his door, clamping his hands over his ears.

He didn't realize at first that the laughter had faded and that he was very close to tears.

"Davey!"

It was Paige. He ignored her. "Davey, can I come in, please?"

"Just go away."

Then he heard somebody clearing his throat, and Justin's growl: "Come on, Jacob, you caused this! Mom is due home any minute!"

"Davey, I'm sorry, I'm really sorry. I mean it. Can we come in?"

Davey hesitated a minute, then walked to the door. The three of them stood there with stricken faces. Something a little bit warm trickled through him. They made fun of him, but they made fun of each other. He was their cousin. They did care.

He smiled slowly. Paige let out a shaky sigh. But Jacob was the one to speak, with wide, earnest eyes. "It's all right if you want to think the Babe comes back to help you,

Davey. You really think a lot of him. You — uh — you got to do whatever helps, right?"

"Right!" Justin, trying to be old, trying to be the mature mediator, answered for Davey.

"Are we all okay?" Paige asked him.

Davey nodded. Yeah, they were okay. But he wasn't going to mention Babe Ruth again, ever.

"All right, then, let's get the table set. Mom will be home any minute." She started to walk away and then turned back. "You know what, cuz?" she said, ruffling his hair. "You *are* the only one really caring about Mom." She stared at her brothers. "Maybe we'll all be that way now, huh?"

"Yeah," Jacob said with an uneasy flush.

They heard the door open and close downstairs.

"Hey, where is everyone?"

Aunt Becky was home. They stared at one another guiltily, then went racing on down the stairs.

"Here! We're all here!" Paige called.

It turned out to be a nice night. A real nice night. Jacob even helped him with his math homework.

It felt almost like home.

Like a family. A real family.

Now . . .

If he could just manage to get Tim into it . . .

If he could just bat! Everything seemed to hinge on whether or not he could bat!

Come back, Davey thought, thinking of the Babe and closing his eyes. Come back, please. I need you. Please! He opened his eyes and stared out the window at the north star, burning very brightly. *Please, I need you. Come back!*

Maybe he would. Maybe Davey just had to believe in the miracle.

Friday was a lousy day. She was busy from seven o'clock on, getting the kids set for school and then getting to work. Christmas was getting hard. She was in high demand.

It was nice. It was also exhausting.

Maxine's was a great place. She loved it. It was elegant, but not uncomfortably so. The booths were very intimate and private.

She couldn't wait to see Tim, but she didn't want to appear too anxious. She had changed from reindeer costume into a simple black dress — basic black, that's what she had always heard looked the best — in a two-by-four dressing room.

She arrived about ten minutes late. Just when she reached the restaurant, she ripped her left stocking.

And then she saw Tim. A buxom blonde was sitting across from him, flirting away.

Becky stood still for just a minute. She swallowed hard. Who was she kidding? The blonde was young. Very.

Her knees felt weak again. There was just no future in this. She was setting herself up for a fall.

Ah, but dinner! People were staring at her in the restaurant's foyer. The hostess was coming toward her.

"I'm meeting a friend," Becky said quickly. She forced a smile. "He's right over there," she said, pointing to Tim's booth.

The woman smiled and nodded. Becky hurried on toward the booth. By the time she got there, the blonde was gone.

"Hi," she murmured, sliding into the seat across from him where the young blonde had been sitting moments before.

He smiled, reaching over the table to take her hand in his, squeezing it. Becky didn't squeeze his fingers in return. He said something to her, but she didn't hear him.

Suddenly Becky was remembering something that had unnerved her confidence not long after they had met the first time. She had been at the field, talking about cars, looking through the classifieds. She had the idea of trying to get a second car for the kids. Mike

Harden's father, Lew, had been there. He'd pointed at her choice of car and hooted, "That's not going to do it, Becky. You need something sharp and sporty, a little two-seater, a Porsche, a Jag — something sexy. And you're going to have to lose the kids, too, Becky. What self-respecting guy is going to pick up an instant nursery school? Men don't like extra baggage, Becky baby — they just like to rock and roll!"

So Lew Harden was a jerk! she told herself furiously now. Becky had no right to hold what Lew said against Tim. But she couldn't help remembering the conversation, and the disasters that had occurred when she had tried getting involved before. Tim was a free agent, no ex-wife, no children. He had a great job and a smile that charmed. There were no pretenses about him, and just by being what he was, he could attract anyone.

As well as those women who would simply be attracted by his fame. There were all kinds of pretty young groupies out there who would go after him just because his face was on a baseball card.

Oh, she had her own version of fame. But she'd never heard of anyone lining up to spend their lives with a tap-dancing reindeer.

"Becky, are you with me?"

She nodded and tried to smile. She was

doing this to herself, she realized, and she just had to get a grip on herself. Even if she couldn't keep him forever, she would have dinner with him, and they would be alone. She needed to smile and have a nice time.

"Yes, I'm sorry." She tried to make her voice light, easy, and casual, and yet sincere.

It was stiff, and he heard the tone.

He leaned back, groaning. A dark brow arched her way. "It was my young friend, right?"

She shook her head, her smile plastered in place. Then she realized he knew she was lying, and she shrugged. She felt compelled to tell him, "You looked good with her."

"She's just an old friend, Becky. We've never dated. I told her that I wasn't alone, that I was waiting for you, and then she went back to work. She's got a Christmas job in the department store."

"I didn't ask you for an explanation."

"No, you just suggested that I should be with her."

"I didn't suggest anything."

"I'm surprised that you didn't run home."

Becky inhaled deeply. The comment had a little note of either sarcasm or bitterness to it. Had he wanted her to run home?

Tim looked great. He wore his suit so well. He wasn't very young, but he was still young, and he was handsome and confident, without being abrasive or arrogant. He was striking, sexy, wonderful.

He even had all his hair.

And it was true, he had looked darned good with the young girl.

She shook her head and tried again to get a grip on her emotions. It was as if she wanted something so badly that she was throwing it away from herself with all her strength at the same time.

"It's just that — this isn't going to work," she told him. Leave, she told herself. With dignity, with a warm thank you — with the truth. *I could have fallen head over heels in love with you, but . . .*

Men didn't like a lot of baggage. And she very passionately loved all the baggage that came with her.

She almost stood then, but his fingers curled over hers, holding them tightly. "Glass of wine?" he asked her.

"I don't know —" she began, but Tim nodded to their waiter just past her shoulder, and the man was now standing at the table. Even if Tim hadn't been holding her hand, she wouldn't have been able to get past the waiter and leave anyway.

"Wine?" he asked her.

Wine, yes. Something, anything. Tonight.

She looked straight at the waiter. "Scotch on the rocks, please," she said flatly.

"Make it two," Tim said, and kept staring at her. Then he leaned back and grinned. "Wow. This is great. I drive you to drink."

Becky blushed. "You don't drive me to do anything —" she began.

"That's right, I don't." He wasn't leaning back anymore. and he wasn't smiling anymore, either. "I don't force you to do anything."

"Tim, we tried this once before. It didn't work. We got into a terrible argument —"

"Whoa, whoa!" he said adamantly. "Let's backtrack. You would only see me when it absolutely fit your convenience. And Becky, things were great. The time we spent alone together was some of the best time I've had in my entire life. Better than a grand-slam home run."

She felt her cheeks growing warm and red. *Their time together had been some of the best she had spent in her entire life, too.*

But there lay the key. The time that they had spent *alone* together, he had said. Without baggage. And no matter how precious that time was to him, he would want more out of life, and she couldn't give it. He would want a weekend in the Bahamas, and she would need to take one of the kids for a scout camp trip into Okeefee Park. And he could say whatever he wanted to say, but eventually Jacob would put a frog in his drink. Or maybe Jacob wouldn't put a frog in his drink, but she'd feed him one burnt meat loaf too many. Or he'd come over before the septic tank was completed and the house would smell like a barn. Something, something awful would happen, and she wouldn't have a thread of pride left.

He would walk away from her.

"Tim," she said softly, and a little bit of the truth did spill disjointedly from her, "That's why this doesn't work. I'm not trying to blame you. I —"

"Becky, you canceled dates all the time."

"I had to, and that's what you can't seem to understand —"

"No, Becky, you never gave me a chance to understand. You never gave me a chance to say, hey, that's fine, or more important, hey, I'd really like to see your son's basketball game."

Their waiter approached their table with their drinks. Suddenly, he seemed to sense some danger in the tone of Tim's voice. Just as he nearly arrived, he dipped around, as if to run away from the table.

But Tim had seen him. "Hey! Come back here with those!" A small, thin Latin man with a curving moustache, he smiled with lips that twitched and put the glasses down as speedily as he could manage.

"What's your name?" Tim asked the waiter.

"Jose," the waiter said quickly.

Tim gave him a tense smile. "Well, Jose, I thought it was me. Now she's driving *me* to drink!" he said woefully.

Becky tried to kick Tim beneath the table. Jose suddenly gasped and hopped backward, dropping his pad as he gripped his shin.

"What — ?" Tim said.

"I'm so, so sorry!" Becky exclaimed, now burning red and deeply embarrassed. How had she missed Tim and kicked the waiter?

Tim was glaring at her, astounded. He bent down for the waiter's pad.

"Reflexes!" Becky told the man quickly. "My leg just — jerked! Really, I'm terribly, terribly sorry."

"No problema, no problema," the waiter said, offering them another smile — his lips were really twitching now. "Have you decided on dinner?" he asked, keeping a safe distance from the table.

"I'm sorry, I've decided I can't —" Becky began, about to say that she just couldn't stay after all.

But Tim didn't give her a chance. "We'll both have the Cajun dolphin platters, please."

"Wait —" Becky began, but even as the nervous waiter stared at her, backing still farther away, Tim cut in again.

"I'm the one paying the bill, and honest, I tip a heck of a lot better than she does. Women — cheap, you know. Hurry up now, she's dangerous as well. Get away from her quick!"

Good old Jose was only too willing to oblige.

"Women! Cheap!" Becky protested furiously. "I've done this for a living, you fool, and I'm always very generous —"

He was leaning across the table again, his hands around hers. "See? I fit right in. You've got — what? Butthead, Dimwit, Numbnutts — and who was the other kid?"

"Idiot, I think, I don't remember. They have new names to shout at one another daily," she said wearily.

"And now you've got Fool," he said quietly.

Becky pulled at her hand. "May I sip my drink, please?"

"I don't know. Are you going to kick me again?"

"I didn't kick you."

"Jose won't be walking right for a week."

"I didn't mean —"

"It's all right. He'll be on guard from now

on. And I'll do my best to protect him."

"Tim —"

"Becky, relax."

He released her, and Becky sipped her Scotch. She moistened her lips. "I'm just trying to explain." She waved a hand in the air. "Tim, you did look good with that young girl. You have everything ahead of you. You should have your own kids. Trust me. Not everyone can deal with a ready-made family. And I — well, I can't deal without it."

He studied her for several long minutes. She grew nervous.

"Tim, you can't tell me that going out with my wild bunch is your idea of a great evening out! You must want to be with someone young and unencumbered and — and I just don't think that you can handle a lifetime of what I've got."

"Maybe I can't," he told her flatly.

She swallowed hard. He was agreeing with her, and she felt as if she had just been slapped. "Well, then you'll understand my position —"

"No, let me tell you what I do understand, Becky. You've made all my judgments for me. We're about the same age, yet somehow you've decided that you're old and I'm young."

"Well, it's true!" she said miserably.

"Haven't you heard? It's not the years, it's the mileage. And I usually feel as if I've been around the world a zillion times. And everyone knows that women age faster."

"Do they? From all the statistics I've seen, women also outlive the hell out of men!" he reminded her. "But men also go bald and get gray hair and balloon guts!" he added cheerfully.

She almost smiled. "Well, they even have spray-on hair for men now —"

"And women. You're not going bald, are you?" he asked.

"No!" she gasped, then realized that he was teasing.

"I wouldn't mind if you were. We could just spray that instant hair of yours on both our heads."

"Tim, you're missing the point. I —"

"Listen to me, Becky. You never gave yourself a chance. And you sure as hell never gave me one."

"I don't know —"

"You never cared enough to give me the benefit of the doubt."

"Never cared enough!" she flared furiously. "Tim — you arrogant fool! Mr. Baseball Hero, with everyone running around him, everyone wanting him. Damn you! I care enough not to ask you to give it all up!"

The waiter was coming with their food. She saw poor Jose out of the corner of her eye, but fear and anger and all the things she didn't want to face were building up inside her. She tried to lower her voice, but it seemed to rise anyway.

Jose reached the table.

Tim slammed his hand upon it. "No, Becky, you never cared enough to credit me with wanting more out of life than a sports car and a blonde."

Jose's twitching smile faded altogether. He tried to swerve away from the table, but Tim, still staring at Becky, was reaching for Jose's tray. "Would you set the damned food down, please!"

"There you go!" Becky claimed heatedly. "You're angry with me, and you're taking it out on poor Jose."

"I'm not the one who halfway crippled the poor man!" Tim claimed.

"You take the food — take it!" Jose said hastily, relinquishing the entire tray to Tim's grasp. Muttering in Spanish, Jose made a quick escape.

Tim, the tray in his hands, sank back down to his seat. "You've lived in central Florida long enough to pick up some Spanish," he told her. "What did our friend Jose say?"

Becky felt her own lips twitching. "I think

he said that he'd tip you to go and have dinner somewhere else." She couldn't help it — she started to laugh. In a moment he was laughing with her. Suddenly it felt wonderful to be with him, and it felt right. She cared about him so very much. And when his eyes touched hers, as they did now, when his eyes were alive with laughter and tenderness, she could almost believe . . .

He cared about her. She didn't doubt that he did. It was just that the entire thing was wrong, and she was going to get very badly hurt. Her laughter faded. He frowned, watching her, realizing that a moment that had been special was now gone.

He groaned and set their plates in front of them. "Becky, you are the most exasperating woman I have ever met!" He stood up and carried the empty tray over to the service stand near their table. A silver-haired lady stared at him. Tim strode back to join Becky at their table.

"You're making a scene," she warned him.

"You kick the waiter, and *I'm* making a scene?" he demanded.

"I didn't *try* to kick the waiter —"

"No, you were aiming at me. And look who's worried about making a scene? The woman who spends half her life in a tomato costume!"

He'd never made fun of her for the strange activities her profession brought about — in fact, she'd always thought he understood and supported her.

"I make a damned good living as a tomato," she countered. She was feeling defensive, and she was instinctively combating her defensiveness with anger. "And I enjoy myself!" she assured him.

"Really? I can't imagine it's that much fun to be a stuffed red ball with twigs in your hair!"

"Actually, Mr. Smart Aleck, I haven't played a dancing tomato in a very long time."

"Oh yes, it's Christmas. Wrong season. You're a dancing reindeer these days."

That stung. She sat back. "Who do you think you are? Just because you used to be a hotshot baseball player —"

"Want to hit any farther below the belt?" he interrupted her tensely.

"No. Do you?"

"Dammit, Becky, no! I'm just trying to shake you up, to make you understand, to see things —"

"I see things just fine, Tim. I see the truth. And the truth is, we just can't do this to each other. I don't want to strike at all, I just —"

She broke off. She could have started laughing, and she could have told him that there were just too many pretty little blondes in the world, and that she . . .

She wanted to believe that she could compete with them. But it just wasn't possible. The more she saw him, the more she cared about him. And the more involved she became . . .

The more shattered she would ultimately be.

She couldn't stay and have dinner. She'd burst into tears, and she'd try to explain it to him, and she'd feel like a fool.

She leaped up. "I'm sorry. I'm truly sorry. I shouldn't have come. Thank you for dinner."

She dropped her napkin on the table and started to hurry from the restaurant.

"Becky!"

She heard him calling her name. Everyone heard him calling her name. It didn't matter.

It was wrong to run.

And still, she was running. Just as fast as she could.

"Becky!"

She turned back. She was at the door, and he was making his way through the crowd to her. But then good old Jose — poor, abused Jose — waylaid Tim, handing him the bill.

Tim took the bill. His eyes met Becky's across the room.

She felt just like Cinderella.

But the clock had struck midnight. And she didn't even have a glass slipper to leave behind.

Maybe that was it. She couldn't get over the feeling that she was living in the ashes while he was in the palace. She wanted the courage to take a chance.

She wanted to believe in herself.

She just didn't know how. Not anymore.

Christmas music was playing loudly from a speaker outside the restaurant. "Jingle Bells." It was Christmas, the time of good cheer.

How could it make her feel so sad?

Bah, humbug. Tim was still staring at her as he dug in his pocket for his wallet. He would pay the bill any second. If she was really going to escape, she couldn't stand here and stare at him while the voice coming over the speakers burst into a cheerful rendition of "Deck the Halls."

She turned and hurried out into the darkness.

Chapter 5

From the window of his room, Davey saw Aunt Becky's car coming into the driveway.

He heard the car door open and then slam.

He looked at the clock on the nightstand by his bed and winced. It was barely nine-fifteen. She hadn't stayed out very long.

Davey kept staring out the window, long after Becky came into the house. He could hear her downstairs, talking to Paige, saying something about making it an early night because she was working again early the next morning. It was a lie, Davey thought. A cheerful lie, to make them all think that she had had dinner with Tim, that it had been a casual, friendly thing and no more, and now she was back.

A second later, he heard a tapping at his door. He opened it quickly. Aunt Becky was there. She looked really nice in a scoop-neck black dress that came just to her knees, high heels, and stockings. She was smiling brilliantly for him, but he thought that her eyes looked damp, as if she'd been crying — or thinking about crying. He knew the feeling. He wondered if Tim had seen them looking like that, and then he knew, no, of course not. Aunt Becky tried never to let anyone see when she was hurting.

"Hey, kiddo. Just came up to see how you're doing," she told him.

"I'm doing fine. But —"

"Last tryout is tomorrow," she said softly. "You've got to get some sleep. That's important."

"I'm going to go to bed in a few minutes," he assured her. "Are you going to be at the park tomorrow?"

She nodded. "I work from eight until twelve. They're opening very early tomorrow since it's the last Saturday before Christmas. I told them four hours and no more, so I'll be there the minute I can change from a reindeer costume to jeans! I know you're going to do okay, though. I just know it."

He doubted it, but he smiled back. "Did you have a nice dinner?" he asked her.

"Um, yes — fine, thank you."

"You came home awfully early."

"Yes, well, you know. Work."

"Right." Davey nodded. He couldn't call his aunt a liar and demand to know what went wrong. He smiled again. She gave him a quick, warm hug. "You just believe in yourself,

Davey. Give it your best and believe in yourself." She broke away, kissed his forehead, and started out of the room.

"Aunt Becky!" he called after her.

She paused in the doorway, looking back.

"Nice dress," he told her. He nodded gravely. "Good legs."

She grinned. "Thanks. Being a dancing reindeer does help keep my weight down," she murmured dryly. "Good night, kiddo. Get some sleep."

She closed the door. Davey fell back on his bed, closing his eyes, almost groaning aloud. They'd gone out — and she'd come right home. What had happened? What had gone wrong? Had it been him? Had they argued over him?

He opened his eyes and nearly screamed out loud, nearly jumped right through the roof.

The Babe was there. George Herman Ruth. Sitting right there in Davey's bedroom, at the foot of the bed. He was staring around the room.

"Nice place, kid," the Babe said, grinning as he studied the life-size poster of himself. "Real nice place you keep."

Davey realized suddenly that the Babe was smoking a cigar. He leaped out of bed and rushed over to snatch the cigar out of his hands, and then he remembered who he was.

"Mr. Ruth — you — you can't smoke a cigar up here! My aunt will smell the smoke. I'm sorry, I'm really sorry —"

"Hey, no problem, kid." The Babe handed the cigar right over. Davey wrinkled his nose and ran into the bathroom with it. He started to throw it down the toilet, then remembered all their septic tank problems and ran it under the faucet in the sink for a moment. Then he wrapped it in tissues and threw it into the trash can. He'd hide it better later.

He came out of his bathroom, half expecting the Babe to have disappeared. After all, it was probably pretty rude to ask the ghost of a legend not to smoke.

But the Babe remained. He was standing in the center of the room, and he had picked up Davey's bat. He was holding it the way he'd been holding his own bat in the picture on the poster on Davey's wall.

"It ain't so much a sport that needs muscle, Davey," the Babe said. "It's watching that ball. Watching it, no matter how fast it's moving. It's knowing when it's a good one. Connecting. You've just to get the feel for connecting. You're a fast kid — and I'll bet once you get to first, you're damn — sorry — darned good at getting around the bases."

"Yeah, I can steal," Davey said proudly. "And I always know when it's a high pitch or a low one." He sighed. "I don't go for the wild ones or the bad ones. I just somehow miss the good ones. And when I do get on base, with half a chance, I can get home. But — well, I know the good balls when I see them. I just miss a few."

"Everybody misses some of the good ones. You've got to remember this — you get three chances. Even if you miss the first two, don't give up. There's going to be that third chance. And you've got to go for it with all the vim and vigor — and the *belief* — that you've gone for the other two. You got that?"

Davey nodded.

The Babe let the bat fall. "What's the matter, kid? You worried about your aunt, huh?"

Davey lowered his head. He lifted his arms with exasperation. "They went out! She should have been gone a long time, but she came right home. And . . ."

"And?"

"She looked like she'd been crying."

The Babe sighed. "Everybody misses a few — and everybody has a bad day now and then, you know."

Davey nodded. "I just can't help but feel that — well, okay, she had three kids on her own. She's always struggling. And now she has me as well, and maybe if I weren't here —"

"You know, kid, you can't take on the weight of the world," the Babe said quietly. "She loves you a lot. And making you happy makes her happy."

"Yeah, all right, but not enough. So I have to try. I have to do something. I just can't let her be tired — and lonely — and alone. They're kind of the same thing, but kind of not."

"You ever heard that expression — you can lead a horse to water, but you can't force it to drink?"

Davey nodded. "Yeah, I've heard the expression. So —"

"She's a good lady, your aunt. A nice one."

"Pretty, too, don't you think so?"

"Mighty pretty. But sometimes, grown-ups can be an awful lot like kids. Sometimes they forget how to believe in themselves. You just keep letting her know that dancing reindeer do have nice legs. And you start believing in yourself, really believing in yourself. Maybe when she sees you doing it, she'll catch on herself."

Davey grinned. "You mean she's afraid —"

"Well, now, I'm just guessing on this situation, but yeah, maybe she's afraid. She wants to go for the team, but she's afraid she isn't going to make it."

"So I've just got to get her to go out for

the team," Davey said. He grinned. "She doesn't have to start out with a grand slam — she just has to get to first base."

"And steal the way home," the Babe agreed.

"If she'll just keep her eye on the ball . . ."

"She needs to get up the courage to try to make the team," the Babe said. "She's got to believe in herself. It's something you've all got to get to in this household, huh?"

"Did you always believe in yourself?" Davey asked him. "Always? Was that a true story about you hitting a homer to right field because you'd promised a little kid in the hospital that you'd do it? Did you really point out to center field — and then smack the ball over the fence?"

The Babe nodded, grinning ear to ear. "Yep. True story. I always liked kids. Kids always liked me. And that kid got better, you know. He came to see me later." He stood in the middle of the room. "I remember that day! Jeez, even now, I can remember the roaring going on in the stadium, people stamping their feet, screaming, shouting. I can see the pitcher, see his mean little face, see him spitting on the ground. And there was the catcher, signaling away, the pitcher shaking his head, nodding — spitting again. And I can remember the feel of the ball when it hit the bat — you know that feeling, Davey? That feeling that comes when you know you got the ball just dead-square perfect solid. You can hear it! Well, I remember knowing that it was a homer. It was good. Hey, maybe it just felt so good that I had to do it over and over again.

"But you know what? You remember this: You can have two strikes against you, and still point out to right field, and send the ball soaring. Hey, it's getting late. Get over here. Time for some last-minute pointers. Most important — eye on the ball. Bend your knees, step into the swing. Level swing, kid. Nice level swing."

"Got it!" Davey said. "Got it!" Wow. The Babe was great. Davey had almost heard the roar of the crowd when the Babe was talking. He'd seen a blue sky, felt the thunder going on in the stands. He could see the mean pitcher — the guy would have looked like an older Mike Harden, with tobacco stains on his teeth — and he would have been tough as nails!

Davey took the bat from the Babe. He listened carefully: he swung at imaginary balls. It seemed that they worked a long time — an exceptionally long time, considering that not once did they use a real ball! — and then at last, the Babe sighed deeply.

"Well, kid, I think we've gone about as far as we can go," the Babe said. He sat down at the foot of Davey's bed again, breathing heavily. "It's up to you tomorrow. You hang in there, you hear?"

Davey nodded gravely. "I'll hang in. No matter what." He hesitated, then asked quietly, "How come they never let you manage a team? That's what you really wanted to do, huh?"

The Babe nodded, then shrugged. "Yeah, that's what I really wanted to do. And I would have been good, real good. It hurt, I'll grant you that. Bad. But then again, I'd had a real good roll at it while I was out there, kid. There was only one Babe Ruth."

"Only one!" Davey assured him. "Only one. You were the greatest. No one has ever forgotten."

The Babe grinned ear to ear again, standing. "You get up there tomorrow, and you believe that you're going to hit that ball. You're a good little player, Davey. More than that, you're a good kid. That's most important. The ball-playing isn't everything in life. Some guys learn that too late."

"I know. I just like playing the game. Getting on the team matters because of Tim and Aunt Becky."

"Well, kid, it's Christmas — you just never know."

"Yeah, well, tonight didn't seem to go so

well for Tim," Davey said, rising. He walked across the room and put his bat in the corner.

When he turned around, George Herman Ruth was gone. He stared about, but his room wasn't that big — and the Babe sure wasn't small. He was definitely gone.

"Am I going nuts?" he asked himself.

He walked into the bathroom and dug into the trash can.

It was still there. The cigar. Some kind of Cuban cigar.

This was Florida. There were all kinds of Cuban things around. . . .

But not cigars. Not in his bedroom. His cousins would think he had been smoking in his bedroom, but Davey knew better.

He walked to the windows and looked out on the night. Christmas was so close. Maybe there *were* Christmas miracles.

Oh, God, please, he prayed in silence. He didn't have words to go with it. His prayers were all in his heart that night.

He turned around, flicked off the light, shimmied out of his jeans, and crawled into bed. He just had to get some sleep.

It was midnight when Becky heard a light tapping on the door.

She should have been asleep herself, but she wasn't. She hadn't been able to sleep. She'd shed her dress and her torn hose and spent a good twenty minutes beneath steaming water, and at last all the knots seemed to leave her neck and shoulders. She'd scrubbed her face and her hair and donned her flannel nightgown with the lace at the collar, and once the kids had all gone to sleep, she'd made herself a hot chocolate and carried it into the living room. She sat staring at the too-big Christmas tree and the gaudy lights that tinged areas of the room red and green and blue and yellow.

The door. The light, light tapping . . .

Tim?

The tapping came a little bit harder, more persistently. Then she knew for sure it was Tim. He was calling out to her.

"Becky, I know you're in there. And I know you're up! Your house is nearly as bright as Rockefeller Center. Becky, if you'd just —"

By that time, she'd stood and made her way to the door.

"Tim, go away!" she moaned.

"Open the door, Becky. I want to talk to you."

"Tim! I'm not a charity case. Please, give yourself a Christmas gift. Go away."

"Becky, open the door."

"Tim, you have a knack for showing up

at my worst moments. Have a heart — leave me some pride. My hair is wet."

"Good. I like clean hair."

"And stringy. Wet and stringy."

"I can deal with stringy."

"I have white stuff all over my face."

"Really? Let me see?"

She hesitated a moment, then threw the door open. He stayed on the porch for a moment, staring at her.

"There's nothing white on your face," he commented after a moment.

She sighed. "Tim —"

"All right. So your hair is stringy."

"Tim!"

"I'm kidding. May I come in? Or are you going to leave me standing out here on the porch?"

"Tim, I knew dinner wouldn't be such a good idea —"

"Okay, dinner is out. How about sex?"

"Tim —"

"Becky, come on! Let me in. I want to talk to you."

"Oh! About Davey —"

"Yes."

She backed up. He came into the house and closed the door behind himself.

"Is there something I should know about tomorrow? I'll be there, of course. Is he — ?"

"Davey will probably do well. How well, we'll have to see."

"But what did you want to tell me about him?"

Tim shook his head. "Nothing."

"But you said —"

"I lied. I didn't want to stand out on your porch."

She sighed softly. "I wish you hadn't come here. You don't understand."

"You're right, I don't."

"But you shouldn't come here."

"Becky, you can't run out on me here. It's your home. So it's a good place to talk."

"Don't count on that. Maybe I will run out. Then you'll be sorry. *You* can deal with my septic tank, and with Butthead, Numbnutt, Idiot, and Dimwit."

He was staring at her. He didn't smile, he just kept watching her. She flushed, looking around, and again felt at a tremendous disadvantage. He still looked like a million bucks: his thick hair waving over his forehead, his fortyish years giving him a handsome maturity instead of crow's-feet and silver streaks, his nicely muscled body dynamite in his casual suit. And here she was, Becky the makeup-less. All right, she didn't have white gunk on her face, but her hair was wet and stringy.

"You know what, Becky?" he said after a moment.

"What?" she asked softly.

"I've had all kinds of surgery on my knee. You've seen it. It looks just like hell."

She arched a brow to him. "What — ?"

"Would you walk away from me because of my knee?" he asked her.

She inhaled and exhaled sharply. "Of course not! But —"

"Becky, no one gets to our age without a few scars."

"So I'm old — and scarred?" she said.

"Dammit, Becky, I like the fact that you move a thousand miles an hour! I like the fact that the kids mean more to you than a night out on the town! I like it that this place looks like a tinsel town for Christmas! And you know what? Mainly, I like you!"

She was startled to realize that he was suddenly walking toward her. With intent. She backed away. Right into the wall. It was where he wanted her. He leaned his hands on the wall at either side of her head and kissed her.

It was a great kiss. And she was too stunned to protest it. It was a long, great, breath-stealing kiss that left her knees feeling like rubber. The magic was back. His kiss instantly reminded her of the nights at his place after dinner out, watching classic old movies, sipping drinks, laughing, talking, kissing, feeling this way, loving the sight, the scent, the touch of a man.

She'd come so close . . .

His lips parted from hers. Her lashes fell over her cheeks as she struggled for something to say.

"Pretty good, huh?" he murmured.

Her eyes flew open. "Pretty egotistical!" she whispered.

"Unh-unh! Actually, darned good. But that's all right. It was just a taste. If you want more, I get an apology first."

"An apology?" she gasped.

"You were absolutely awful at dinner."

"*I* was! You were the one who nearly sent that poor waiter flying back to communist Cuba!" Becky accused him.

"You kicked him. You were driving me nuts!"

"Me —"

"Over that blonde."

"Will you please get out of here?" she demanded, aggravated.

"Hey, don't you have kids sleeping in here?" he asked, his voice level and low, making her feel all the more the fool.

"Yes, I have kids sleeping! And you really ought to give me some warning before you come here to pick fights —"

"If I warned you, Becky, I'd never get in this place. And, after all, it's only fair. You're so worried about the truth all the time. Well, I've seen the truth. And for no makeup and stringy hair, you still look pretty good. I mean, I can imagine a whole lot worse in the morning than what I'm seeing now."

"Oh!" she gasped. "Oh! You are really something!" She shoved against his chest and started past him, quickly, angrily, her heart thundering. She strode past and found herself out on the porch.

"Becky." He'd followed her. Complacent. He seemed perfectly pleased with himself this evening. "It's your house, remember?"

"Good. Then you get out of it!" she shouted.

"Shh! Kids are sleeping, remember?"

"Tim, if you don't —"

"I'm going," he said pleasantly.

"Why on earth did you come?"

"I wanted you to remember what you were missing." He walked away from the house at last, but then he paused. "I sure did a lot of remembering tonight. Remember the tacos in the bathtub?"

"Will you please go?" she whispered almost desperately.

"I'm going. I'm going. I just thought I

should let you know something."

"And what's that?"

The teasing nonchalance left his voice, and when he stared at her again, it was with a certain tension in his features. "I was falling in love with you, Becky. Yeah, maybe it would have been better if I'd fallen for someone twenty-eight, single, and employed by IBM or Triple A! But that's not how life works. Things aren't all red roses around here, but Becky, you never gave me credit. I like kids. Your life is wild, but it's also warm."

"Tim —"

"That's it. I'm leaving. No more groveling. I just wanted to make sure that you remembered the tacos in the bathtub — and kissing. Now that you do, it's in your hands. I'm going, and if you want more of anything that I've got to give, well, then, Rebecca Wexham, you can just come to me! And *you* can do a little bit of groveling! I deserve it."

"It will be a cold day in hell —"

" 'Night, Becky," he told her, and coolly walked off the porch, slid into his meticulous car, gunned the motor — and drove away.

She stood on the porch, staring after him. She blinked, unable to believe how he had just come and gone.

"Ahem!"

She heard a throat being cleared behind her.

She turned around quickly and saw Davey standing on the stairs. She closed the door swiftly, twisting the bolts and speaking fast and far too breathlessly.

"Davey! It's so late! What are you doing up? Especially when tomorrow is such a big day. I —"

"I heard a car."

"Oh."

"It was Tim?" Davey asked.

She nodded. "I forgot my sweater in his car," she lied. She winced. Grown-ups weren't supposed to lie like that.

"I'll just get a drink of water," Davey said.

"Right," Becky agreed, "and get back into bed."

He nodded and turned to the kitchen. "Aunt Becky?"

"Yeah?"

"You've really got great legs, you know."

"What?" she asked.

"Great legs. You looked great, all dressed up like you were tonight."

"Oh, thanks."

"You look good in a flannel nightshirt, too. Honest."

She lowered her head, smiling. "Thanks, Davey." He was the world's greatest kid. He'd tell her she looked great if she were a potato in a potato sack. "Come on now, get your water and get to bed."

"Sure." He started for the kitchen, then turned back. "Aunt Becky?"

"Yes?"

"Where is it?"

"Where's what?"

"Your sweater."

"My — sweater. Oh. I guess I put it somewhere — Davey, you know, it really is late."

He was grinning rather happily. "Yeah, I know. It's late." He started for the kitchen one more time, then turned back again. "Aunt Becky, you know, you've got to admit that you want to be on the team!"

"What?"

"Never mind. I'm going to bed." But he hesitated again, then rushed out with, "If you don't take a swing at it, you'll never hit the ball!"

Suddenly, he was all motion, flushing, hurrying away from her and into the kitchen.

She leaned against the locked door.

He was right. So very right.

She was the one who kept talking to him about trying. About playing his best.

And she wasn't even willing to get up to bat herself.

Oh, God, what was she to do now?

Nothing. She had to get to bed herself. She had to be a reindeer tomorrow. Then she'd have to hurry up and get to Davey's last try-out.

She was going to go to bed.

And damn Tim!

She just wasn't going to dream about tacos in the bathtub!

Becky started up the stairs, heading to her own room. In the hallway, she paused. Davey's light was still on. She tapped on the door, twisting the knob. "Davey —"

She broke off. Davey was sitting on his bed, a half-smoked cigar in his hands. He had been studying it as if the darned thing were a text-book. She never just opened a door on the kids, but tonight she had. And she hadn't given him a chance to hide the cigar.

Cigar? Davey?

But in fact, the room seemed to carry the smell of it.

"Davey?" she said, arching a brow.

"Aunt Becky," he said. She wasn't sure if he sounded guilty or not.

"Davey, that's a cigar," she said.

He nodded. "Yeah, it is!" he said enthusiastically.

Stunned, she leaned against the doorframe. "Davey, you know that no one smokes in this house, except an occasional guest. You're way too young, and —"

"Oh, no, Aunt Becky. I wasn't smoking.

It's the Babe's cigar."

She inhaled and exhaled, wondering if she hadn't let him take the Babe Ruth thing just a little bit too far.

"Davey, it sure does smell like that cigar has recently been smoked. But Babe Ruth is dead."

He stood up, still holding the dirty old brown thing as if it were a priceless relic.

"Aunt Becky," he said indignantly, "I do not smoke."

The core of indignant honesty in his words brought a smile curving into her lips. "Then you listen to me, young man. If you're trying to protect one of your delinquent cousins —"

"No, no! Honest!" he cried quickly. "Aunt Becky, the cigar really *was* the Babe's. I swear it. I'll swear it on a Bible if you want."

She hesitated, wondering if she should be worried about him.

"Davey, I always trust you to tell me the truth," she said softly.

"I am telling you the truth."

She nodded. "All right, then. It was Babe Ruth's."

"Aunt Becky, I know that this doesn't look good. I really wish you would trust me on this one."

She was tempted to smile again. What was the story with the cigar? Was she imagining the smell of smoke just because she was looking at the darned thing?

"What are you doing with it?"

"Putting it up on my shelf, by the cap," Davey told her.

She opened her mouth again. She had a whole list of questions, such as what made him think that he had Babe Ruth's cigar, and how had he come about acquiring it?

But she didn't ask any more questions. Davey needed a few dreams.

Didn't they all?

"Davey, there's just one thing about the Babe's cigar," she told him.

"Yes, Aunt Becky?"

"It better not get lit again."

"Never!" he vowed fervently.

"Good night, then," she said softly. She closed his door and walked down to her own room. She leaned against the door. Dear Lord, but they were a mess!

Davey was revering a cigar. And she, despite her best efforts, would be having all kinds of dreams about tacos in a bathtub.

Chapter 6

"What is he doing? Just what *is* he doing?" Paige demanded irately. She'd been ready to swing at the ball Jacob was about to pitch to her.

Justin was behind her, playing catcher. Davey was about three feet off the doormat that was second base, ready to run for third. Aunt Becky had already been at the mall for at least an hour, and since Davey didn't have to be at the park until twelve, Justin had taken charge and formed a family delegation to do some practicing with Davey before tryout time.

But now Paige was suddenly in rebellion. She stepped out of the batter's box and stared at Justin behind the bundled-up old towel that signified home base. "I want to know what he's doing!"

"What? What? What am I doing?" Jacob demanded irritably. "I'm pitching the ball, that's what I'm doing! And you're supposed to swing the bat at it — and try to hit it!" When he finished his speech, he spat, then started a windup.

"That! That!" Paige cried out, pointing to him wildly.

Davey sighed and walked back to hunker down at second base — waiting. "You mean spitting?" Jacob said incredulously.

"I'm not playing if you're going to spit!" Paige announced.

The boys all stared at one another blankly. Justin stood wearily. "Paige, pitchers spit. It's kind of part of the whole thing."

"I thought pitchers chewed tobacco!" Paige said stubbornly. "That little runt out there throwing the ball at me isn't going to do it with spit all over it."

"I'm not spitting on the ball!" Jacob protested indignantly. He looked at Justin again. "If I can't spit, I can't pitch. Just can't do it."

"Paige, honest, he's not spitting on the ball. I swear it," Justin told his sister.

"I will now!" Jacob called.

"All right, all right!" Justin snapped. "Jacob, get out of there. I'll pitch."

"I'll keep pitching. And I won't spit. Hell, it won't matter with Paige anyway, she couldn't hit the wide side of a barn!" Jacob cried.

Paige stepped back into the batter's box, her eyes narrowed, mean-looking.

Jacob looked mean, too. His teeth were grating so hard that Davey could hear the noise all the way at second base. Davey moved off the base, his hands in the air, getting ready to steal if the catcher lost the ball or moved too slowly with it. He tried to imagine that there were more players in the field. He reminded himself that his speed was one of his strengths.

Jacob wound up and sent the ball flying at his older sister. It whizzed right by her.

"Ball!" Justin called.

"Ball!" Jacob protested. "Ball, my —"

"I'm telling Mom about your language!" Paige warned him.

Jacob's eyes narrowed further. "Ball, my *eye!*" he snapped.

"Come on, come on, we've got to get Davey back up to bat," Justin said.

Jacob wound up again. He sent the ball flying.

It was a hard pitch, a fast pitch, and there was even a curve on it.

Paige nailed it. Davey remembered the Babe talking about how good it felt when the ball and the bat connected like that, making that sound.

It sailed way over Jacob's head, far into the next yard.

Paige dropped the bat. "Yes!" she cried,

fists bunched high to the sky and then to her sides as she danced around the base. "Yes! It's a homer, I think. Over the wall, right into the crowd. Davey, get moving! I think I get to move around the bases however slowly I darn well feel like it, while my team cheers me on and Jacob's team boos the pitcher."

Jacob stared at Justin. "Do I have to put up with this sh—"

"Don't say it, *baby* brother," Paige warned.

Jacob threw down his glove in sheer disgust.

"I'll get the ball," Davey said, and ran after it. When he came back, Jacob was about to walk off the field.

"This is for Davey, remember?" Justin was charging him. "Paige is outfield now. Just pitch to Davey. And make them hard and fast. They'll throw that little pig-nosed Mike Harden at him today, and the kid's an as— the kid's a jerk, but he can pitch. So let's go. Let's move it, move it!"

"All right, all right," Jacob grumbled.

Davey picked up his bat and stepped into the batter's box. Jacob screwed up his eyes, made a face, and spat.

"Tell him to stop that!" Paige said.

"I ain't pitching to you anymore. I'm pitching to the kid here, and he may be a cousin, but he isn't a whiny *girl!*"

"Just throw the ball!" Justin bellowed.

Jacob threw it. Hard, fast — but high. Davey held steady. "Ball!" Justin cried, throwing it back.

Jacob wound up again. The pitch was good. Smooth, clean — right over the plate. Davey could see it coming.

Watch it, watch it, watch it . . .

He swung. His bat whirred through the air. Nothing more.

"Strike!" Justin called. "One and one. Let's go now, let's go."

The next two were good. And Davey watched them. Watched them and knew they were good. He was too tense, swinging too late. Justin called, "Strike three!" Davey stood there, his bat down, his shoulders slumped.

"Even Paige hit the ball!" he said.

"What do you mean, *even* Paige hit the ball?" Paige demanded.

"You wouldn't understand," Jacob told her. "It's a *guy* thing — like spitting!"

"Gee. Actually *hitting* the ball must be a *girl* thing, then!"

"Paige!" Justin roared.

"Hey, Davey, get yourself a real pitcher, and you'll hit the ball," Paige said. "I'm going in. I've had enough."

She swung around. Rear end swaying, she walked off the front-yard field and started toward the house. Then she stopped walking suddenly, staring down the street. A BMW was coming their way.

The boys left their places in the yard as well, walking up to Paige, waiting with her as the BMW pulled into the drive. Tim got out of the car, grinning as the three boys curiously followed Paige up to meet him.

"Hi, coach!" Justin called.

"Hi, Mr. Yeagher," Paige said. "Did you come for Davey? Isn't it a little bit early?"

Tim shook his head, smiling at Davey. "I was going to come back for you if you wanted, Davey. I came to see you, Paige. Or Justin."

"Yeah?" Paige said curiously.

"Could one of you guys stay home tonight? I wanted to ask your mom out again, and I know she won't come if she's worried about the little ones."

"Oh, Jeez, I am not little!" Jacob groaned.

"You're not quite twelve. You won't qualify for voting for a while yet," Tim told him, grinning.

Jacob shuffled his feet. Davey just stared at the man in disbelieving silence.

Three strikes, and you're out, Davey thought. But you just needed to whack one of the three balls that the pitcher had to put right over the plate. That's what Aunt Becky always called to him; *You just need one, Davey, you just need one!*

Well, maybe Aunt Becky needed a few chances, too. And she just needed to really grab one of them.

"I'll be here," Paige assured Tim.

"I thought you had a date with a basketball *hunk!*" Justin said, and added nobly, "I'll be here."

"You were going out with the cheerleader with the *great buns!*" Paige reminded him sweetly.

"I'll make it another time," Justin said pleasantly, "since the cheerleader seems to think I'm a hunk myself."

"Yeah, or Paige can break her date, since I'm sure she thinks she's got *great buns* herself," Jacob said innocently.

Paige gritted her teeth and sighed with exaggerated patience. "Do you think Jacob is returnable, or that we could exchange him or something? Maybe we could get ourselves a little dimwit that actually worked now and then!"

"Hey!" Davey snapped. They'd all been doing so well, almost giving Tim the impression that they could be — good. "They'll both be home, coach. They're both just the wonders of the high school world, and both their dates will be glad to go out with them some other night. Justin will make it up to his girl. He'll actually pay when they go out. And

Paige will make it up to her guy — she'll be ready on time, and she'll actually be nice to him and she won't try to refix his hair all night!"

"Hey!" Paige protested.

But then she fell silent, as did her brothers, just staring at Davey.

Jacob started to laugh. "Hey, you're not half bad after all, butthead!" he complimented.

"Don't you dare call him butthead on that field this afternoon!" Paige warned severely.

"I won't," Jacob said, then added with a grin, "that's a family kind of a thing."

Davey suddenly felt all right. He'd missed all three pitches and Paige had nailed the ball, but he felt all right.

"So, are we settled?" Tim asked.

"Yep, you're on, coach!" Justin assured him.

"Davey, I'll come back for you in about an hour," Tim told him.

Davey shook his head. "No, thanks, coach. I think I should walk over. The other kids, you know."

"Oh." Tim nodded. "Then I'll see you there." He got back into his BMW and drove off.

"Come on, let's practice awhile longer," Jacob told Davey.

"Hey," Paige said, "do you think Mom will

blow it again tonight?"

"I sure as hell hope not!" Justin said, and stared at Davey, shaking his head. "Somehow, this little butthead got things going for her. Tim's really an all right kind of guy."

"All right!" Paige protested. "He's — he's great."

Jacob laughed. "As Mom might say, his BVDs seem to be in the right place, at least. Come on, let's play ball."

They walked back into the yard.

Even Paige.

The mall was a zoo. It was the last Saturday before Christmas. Tim drove around the parking lot twice, watching people battling one another over parking places, honking — even stopping their cars to get out and yell at one another.

He eyed a car that was just pulling out of one of the last rows and drove quickly toward it. But coming at him from the opposite direction was an old Volkswagen Bug. He hadn't seen one in ages, but here was one just about to take his spot. He had the edge, he thought. He realized he was revving his motor and getting ready to floor it just as if he were jousting with the Bug at a tournament with lances and swords.

He brought the BMW to a halt just as the

Bug screeched to a stop as well. He saw the Bug's door open, and he opened his own, prepared for a shouting match.

But the driver of the Bug was a fresh, freckled-faced red-haired girl, around twenty or twenty-one. She didn't yell, she didn't argue.

She just pleaded.

"Oh, mister, I've just got to get in there quickly. I've got to get home to sit with my sister, my mother is sick, and the cat died last night. Oh, Lord! And I had a flat tire on the way here already. I really need to get a kitten quickly — you know, with a big bow around its neck, and I can write a letter from Santa saying that this little cat needs love, too —"

"It's yours," Tim told her.

"What?" she said, stunned.

"The space. Take the space. I'll back up and let you in."

"Oh! Oh, wow! Thanks!" she said. "Thank you so much, oh, thank you —"

"Hey! 'Tis the season!" he called to her, leaping back into the BMW. But the girl didn't get back into the Bug. She stared at him and then came running after the car. "Hey! I know you! You're famous. You used to play something, right? Basketball, football —"

"Baseball," Tim said.

He looked around, wincing. There were cars behind him now, and more cars behind the Bug. Beeping big time.

"Baseball," Tim repeated quickly. "You'd better take that space and we'd both better get out of here —"

The sweet little freckle-faced thing straightened suddenly, her small hands balled into fists as she stared at the beeping motorists. "Hey, take a pill, guys. What is this — male Christmas PMS?" She leaned back down to Tim. "You do the news. The sports news. I watch sometimes. Not sports. Just the sports news." She offered him a vivacious smile. "Ex-jocks can be so cute! You're Tim Yeagher, right? Can I have your autograph? On anything — oh, please? My brother would be just thrilled."

This was it. This sweet, young, addle-brained little creature was what Becky thought he should be looking for in life.

But she was a cute kid, and a fighter. "Your brother?" he asked her skeptically. "But the cat died on your sister, right?"

"Mister, I've got a couple of each, and I'm the oldest of the lot, and let me tell you, going to college is a whole lot easier than coming home. Please, can I have your autograph?"

"May I," Tim murmured.

"What?"

"Never mind." The beeping was getting really loud. Emergency vehicles would come and plow them off the road if they didn't move soon. He found a roster sheet for the afternoon in his glove compartment, ripped off the bottom blank half, and scrawled out his name.

"Oh, thank you —" the girl began again.

"Sure. Merry Christmas. And please, get into the parking space! These people are going to start shooting any minute!"

The girl grinned and hurried back to the Bug. Tim was glad the BMW was an easily maneuverable car, since he had to back up almost to the chrome of a belligerent black Bronco. The Bug pulled into the parking space. He started his weary trek back through the endless rows of parked cars. But just as he started driving, a man walked in front of him with a Burger King bag and cups in his hand. Tim slammed on the brake, recognizing Freddy Maghan, the mall manager. The guy looked frazzled, big time.

But Freddy, so bald that his domed head shone in the Florida December sunlight, seemed glad to see Tim — and not at all aware that Tim had very nearly run right over him.

"Hey, Tim! Pull around back. Take my spot — my kid's got my car and won't be back for me until midnight tonight!"

"Thanks, Freddy!"

Freddy leaned into the BMW's window, shaking his head. "Saw you give the kid the other space."

"Her cat died," Tim said.

Freddy shrugged. "Good story."

"It might have been true."

Freddy grinned. The people behind Tim started beeping again.

"I'd better move," Tim said.

Freddy grinned, straightened, and shook his Burger King bag at the guy in the next car. "Hey, buddy, take a hike, huh?" He sauntered between the parked cars. Tim grinned and smoothly came around the rows of parked cars to reach the reserved employee parking.

He saw Becky's old Volvo, and he found himself just sitting in the car, smiling. There were books piled up in the back, clothes lay about the vehicle — it was very definitely lived-in.

Somehow, Becky just couldn't seem to comprehend that he *liked* her messy car and her chaotic life. He remembered how they had met, literally crashing into each other at the TV station. Everything had flown everywhere, and he sure couldn't have told whether he'd crashed into her or she into him, but she had been instantly apologetic, trying to pick up his things and not in the least aware that she might have gotten hurt herself. She had bent down to gather papers, then had looked up at him. He never knew what it was at that moment that had so attracted him. Great eyes, maybe. Big green eyes that widened as they met his.

"Tim Yeagher, the baseball player. What a great season right before your —" and she had broken off. Right before his knee got busted. He'd been going for some records. Well, those new records weren't going to be set. He'd been bitter at first, and then he'd realized that he had been lucky, he'd had a damned good run at pro ball, and offers were pouring in from across the country for his services as a sportscaster. He'd picked this town south of Orlando mainly because he liked the concept of Florida — his knee ached in cold weather, and although he considered today's high-sixties temperature not quite warm, it was a whole lot better than the twenty below elsewhere.

Hampton City was a nice town, small enough to know people, big enough that they didn't need to know everything about you. He'd been amazed at how swiftly he'd settled in. And then he'd met Becky. He remembered smiling when he'd first seen her. He'd been so surprised that she had known not only who he was but what he had almost done.

"You're up on sports, huh?" he'd asked, grinning.

She'd shrugged. "I never was. But I have kids. Little League, and the like. I find myself watching in sheer self-defense."

He'd noticed the ring on her finger. A plain gold band.

"Is your husband a sports fan?" he'd asked.

"Oh, he was," she'd said softly. "But he's — dead."

"I'm so sorry —"

"Don't be." She'd given him that dimpled grin he'd come to know so well. "It's been some time now. And I have a wonderful family."

"Are you working for the station?" he'd asked her. He had only a few minutes left before he had to be in his seat in front of the cameras.

"No. I was just interviewed. *Working Women.*"

"Oh, yeah. Great."

"It was wonderful to meet you," she said, and he suddenly knew that he didn't want her to walk out of his life. She started by him, and he reached for her arm. The papers flew all over the ground again. She looked at him, and they both started laughing and picked the papers up again. "Have dinner with me later. Drinks. Coffee. Something."

"Oh, I don't know —"

"I'll call you, then."

"No, um — dinner would be great."

And dinner had been great. And everything else that they did together had been great, too. But Becky had held him at a distance. Sometimes she'd gotten animated, broken her shell. Then she'd talked about her family, her late husband, and her brother, and she'd talked a lot about the kids and Davey, and then she'd apologized for talking so much about kids and the trivial little problems in her life. And then she'd clammed right up, and the barriers rose, and the distance was there again. He knew that she did some financial struggling.

At first he wondered if the limp that was always with him, no matter what he did, affected her feelings for him. But then — too late — he'd realized the truth.

Becky didn't mind his limp. She thought of herself as the one limping through life. He'd realized that when they'd had that terrible argument, when she'd tried to run out on him. He'd suggested that maybe she needed to let the children manage a little on their own. She'd replied that he didn't have to be responsible — but she did. And he'd gotten frustrated and told her to run back to the kids — and hide behind them, if that was what she felt she had to do. After she had gone, he realized she was afraid.

And when he thought about it, he really did understand. He'd heard some of the fathers teasing her at baseball, about the things she needed to be fully equipped in the dating field. She didn't sit around and feel sorry for herself, she was in constant, busy motion, but it seemed she had decided there were certain things — such as a life for herself! — that she couldn't have, and so she wouldn't bother to try.

He just wished there was some damned way to make her realize that he didn't find the fullness of her life and its responsibilities to be any more of a hindrance than his knee was to her. She'd refused to see him after that argument. And once again, she'd run out on him last night.

So things were hectic, and maybe he was a little scared about taking on a family. But that didn't mean that he didn't want to — or that he could care about Becky any the less because she loved her children. If only . . .

He was parked, he realized. He got out of the car, locked it, and slipped through the back entrance to the mall. He had two strikes against him, he told himself.

This last swing had to be the good one.

He strode down to the center of the mall by the big fountain where Santa's cardboard house had been constructed. He saw the dancing reindeer out in front right away. Four of them sang and tap-danced away. Holiday shoppers, weary from their struggle to get to the front of the line to pay for their purchases, were happy to pause for a few minutes, grin like idiots — and remember that Christmas was special for children. The show was cute, Tim thought, and a darned good idea. Nothing heavy. You didn't have to see the beginning, and you didn't have to see the end. It was just a little entertainment in the middle of the mall. A good marketing technique.

Except, as he watched the dancers, he realized that none of them was Becky. He frowned for a moment, then waited until the reindeer stopped dancing. He recognized Julie Huggins, a friend of Becky's, twenty-eightish, who was going for her doctor's degree in art history and doing whatever it took to make it through school. She saw Tim as she reached for a towel. "Looking for Becky?"

"Yeah, where is she? I thought she was a tap-dancing reindeer today."

Julie grinned. "Yeah, she was a reindeer for the first hour, but then Santa arrived." She wrinkled her nose. "He'd been celebrating a little early and asked a kid if he wanted a nice bottle of Jack Daniel's in his stocking. Needless to say, that Santa is gone. They've called for another, but in the meantime, one of us had to be Santa, and — well, Becky volunteered. She's a much better Santa than I am. She actually likes those little urchins."

Tim grinned. "Yeah, she does."

"If you want to talk to her, you'd better get in line," Julie warned.

Tim walked around to the line by Santa's house, and his heart sank. There was quite a line of kids there, waiting. He glanced at his watch. He didn't have much time left. He couldn't be late for the tryout. As one of the coaches, he had to see everything that went on. That way, too, he'd be in the best position to fight for Davey.

As he stood there, he saw Freddy Maghan, the mall manager, again. Freddy was still drinking his Burger King Coke, watching the lineup to Santa.

Tim strode over to him casually. "Have you got any pull in Santa's house, Freddy?"

Freddy arched a brow.

"I need to talk to Becky. For just a minute."

"Oh, yeah, sure! Hang on!"

Freddy wasn't subtle. He went right through the line of parents and kids. "Make way here for just a minute. Make way. Message for Santa. It'll be a quick one."

Tim followed Freddy up the steps to Santa's little house, despite the "Heys!" and groans he heard. He almost laughed out loud when he saw Becky — she was stuffed to the gills. Her face had all but disappeared in the midst of Santa-face fur. She was wearing big patchy white eyebrows, and he wouldn't have recognized her in a thousand years.

"Take it easy, kids," Freddy said jovially. "This is Tim Yeagher, the ball player, and he's got a big day at Little League ahead of him."

"Yeagher!" He heard his name called. He felt a little like a fool himself. No, a lot. But he'd come this far. He turned around and waved to the crowd. His eyes fell on a man with a big camera, standing just beyond the kids. It was Jerry Kelly, a free-lance photographer who did a lot with the local paper.

"Look at that!" Jerry called out, waving. "Even the big kids come to Santa for help! What are you asking for, Tim? Take a seat on Santa's lap and let us know!"

The flash went off.

"Hey, kids! Let him get his minute with Santa — then you can all ask him for autographs. Anybody got their baseball cards handy?"

Becky must be just about to die, Tim thought. She'd be jumping up and running away from him — and her job — any second.

He sat quickly right on Santa's lap. He heard a gasp and a groan escape her.

"What in God's name are you doing here?" she demanded.

"I wanted to talk to you."

"Talk! Quickly! With an audience in the hundreds, you realize."

"Yeah, well, I didn't exactly plan this — you're supposed to be tapping with Rudolph over there."

"What do you want?"

"Dinner. Tonight. My place."

"Do you know that you are heavy! You must weigh over two hundred pounds —"

"Two-twenty, to be exact."

"Will you get up, please?"

He shook his head. "I haven't gotten what I came for yet."

"We don't always get what we want. Supposedly, we do get what we need. Now, if you'll only —"

"No, you tell me. What does Santa want for Christmas?"

"Lighter kids. Will you please get up? You're crushing me. And I can't afford to be fired. Santa's busy working on her Christmas septic tank. Will you please — ?"

"Dinner, my house, tonight. And you don't run out."

"Tim —"

"Don't forget, Davey has an important tryout in about, oh, an hour or so."

She gasped. "That's blackmail!" Her eyes narrowed beneath her bushy white Santa brows. "You wouldn't. I know you, and you wouldn't do anything like that."

"Don't be so sure. There's a lot you don't know about me, Becky. You want to take chances with Davey's future?"

"Tim, I don't need dinner —"

"Fine. Just come over to fool around, then."

"Tim! I have the kids —"

"Becky, Paige and Justin are staying home with the younger guys. My house. Seven. I mean it — be there."

Another flash. Jerry Kelly's camera went off a second before he stood. Tim ignored it and started down the steps. "Mr. Yeagher, please!" said one of the kids in line. "Could we get some autographs?"

He glanced at his watch, his heart sinking. "Yeah, I can do a few," he said.

He started to sign. Brand-new baseballs that mothers had in their shopping bags — no longer surprises for the kids' Christmas stocking, but what the heck. He signed bits of paper.

And one lady's shirt.

Finally, he managed to escape, waving to the crowd.

Freddy Maghan waved to him, too. "Hey, Tim! Thanks, thanks a lot!"

He nodded and hurried down the hallway, out to his car. Not bad. He'd reached her. He'd bribed her.

He'd sat on Santa's lap, and she would probably be ready for battle when he saw her again.

Grinning, he started out of the mall parking lot, not even minding the gridlock he hit trying to reach the road out.

He pulled into the baseball field's parking lot about twenty minutes late. Stepping from his car, he could just see field four, and he could see Davey.

He was up at bat. Facing Mike Harden.

The kids had been split up into teams. For the final tryout, they were playing a practice game. The kids would have to field, have to bat, have to make it around the bases. Everything, just like a real game.

Though Mike Harden could be a lot to swallow, he was a good little pitcher. Nasty as all hell, and doing his darnedest to make mincemeat of the kids that came up to bat.

Like Davey. Right now.

Tim ran toward the field. His knee buckled

on him, and he struggled to catch his balance. He slowed to a fast walk and hurried as quickly as he could to the field, his coaching tips all in his head.

Step into it, Davey, kid, think hard, play smart, choke up, step into it . . .

Chapter 7

Becky pulled her Volvo into the parking lot of the field just in time to see Tim running awkwardly toward the field where the tryout was going on. She frowned, pulling off a white brow from her Santa costume as she parked, trying to see why he was hurrying.

Then she saw that Davey had just come to bat.

She jerked off the second white brow with a breathy grunt of pain, brought the Volvo to a halt, and took a second to check her face for stray patches of white. She'd shed the eighteen million little pillows and the Santa suit at the mall and ripped off the big white beard the second she'd gotten into the car. She'd almost forgotten the brows.

She threw the door open now, slammed it, and ran toward the field herself.

Mike Harden was pitching. Naturally. The coaches would use their best pitcher against these kids, knowing they'd be up against the very best pitchers from other Florida teams.

Mike was good, he was even a decent

enough kid — when his father wasn't busy telling him that he was great and the other kids didn't matter. The problem with Mike was that Davey seemed to have a thing about him. Davey had hit off better pitchers — she'd seen him. But Mike had a way of looking at the kid he was pitching to that was downright frightening.

In fact, Becky thought at times, that look was better than his pitch.

"Davey," she said out loud, panting as she neared the field. He couldn't hear her, of course. She walked around the bleachers in front of about two dozen parents, not seeing any of them. She stopped behind the fence, her fingers curling around the links, and looked onto the field. She wanted to talk to him. She wanted to tell him to try his hardest, but to remember that if he didn't make the team, it didn't matter, he had tried his hardest, and that was always what counted most.

She wasn't sure why that was so, she told herself dryly. She conjectured that it was because if you tried your hardest, you never had to wonder later "what if."

She opened her mouth to call to him, then shut it. Tim had called him out of the batter's box and over to the side. She watched Tim give him last-minute instructions. What to watch for, what not to fall for. Davey stood there, nodding gravely at everything Tim said.

He stepped up to bat. Tim walked back to the fenced dugout where some of the other kids waited their turns. He stood in the entrance, staring intensely at Davey.

"Batter up, batter up!" the ump called.

Davey stepped into the box. Mike Harden smiled his wicked, wicked grin. He rolled the ball in his hand, and he spat into the dirt.

Davey looked at Tim, who gave him some kind of a sign. Mike Harden looked at the catcher, and the catcher made signals. Mike shook his head. The catcher gave him another signal. Mike nodded.

"Come on, Mikey — strike him out!" someone shouted from the stands.

"Come on, Davey — cream him!" Becky heard herself shouting back.

The first pitch came flying.

It flew right by Davey, right into the catcher's waiting mitt.

"Strike one!" the umpire called.

"Hey, kid — a buck if you hit it!" someone shouted.

"Hey, Mike — a buck if you strike him out!" Harden's father called.

Becky felt her fingers tighten their grip around the links of the fence.

"Come on, Davey — you can do it!" she

heard. The encouraging words came from one of the kids in the dugout. Becky smiled, glad for the support Davey was getting from friends. "Choke up now, Davey, choke up!" the kid called.

Davey gave no indication that he heard anything going on around him. He looked at Tim and confirmed some kind of signal Tim gave him by passing his nose with his knuckles. Davey nodded, then stared at Mike Harden.

And Mike Harden grinned. Wickedly.

He wound up, and the ball came flying. Davey held dead still. The ball sailed by, but the ump stretched his hand out and Becky breathed more easily. Ball. "Outside, outside!" the umpire called.

Please, Davey, please, Becky prayed. God help him, please, help him. I know that there are people in terrible need, and that we're really very lucky, but Davey still needs this.

Mike didn't like the call on his pitch. He spat twice. He wound up his arm and hurled a fast ball straight at Davey. Davey took a swing. . . .

The ball landed in the catcher's mitt. Now Mike Harden grinned from ear to ear. Two strikes, one ball. Mike Harden — Little League pitcher extraordinaire, in his and his father's minds, at least — was way ahead.

Davey set out a hand, stepped out of the

batter's box, and took a practice swing.

Suddenly Becky felt as if her heart had stopped because he turned, as if instinctively, and saw her standing there. He grinned and gave her a thumbs-up sign.

She smiled broadly and returned it.

"You just need one, Davey, you just need one!"

He nodded to her. He looked at Tim, grinned, and nodded again. Suddenly, he pointed out to left field, still grinning.

"Yeah, yeah, Davey, you gonna get it out there?" Mike Harden called, cackling.

"Hey! None of that!" cried one of the coaches.

"Watch it, Mike," Davey called, his voice light. "When I hit that ball, it might take the hair right off your chin."

"Yeah, right, Larson!" Mike called back.

"Play ball!" roared the ump.

Davey stepped back into the box. He held his bat high, off his shoulder, swinging slightly, his eyes hard on Mike.

Mike wound up. The ball came flying like a white missile out of the sky.

Davey swung.

Becky heard the crack as the bat connected with the ball. Then she saw the white ball flying. Dear God, what a hit! It sailed high and clear and fast. She watched it fly straight toward left field, right where Davey had been pointing.

Becky shouted, screamed, jumped up and down at the fence. "All right, Davey, all right!"

It was going, going . . . gone. Over the fence, out into the street. Davey moved around the bases, running hard for the first three. Then he realized that his ball was completely gone and he trotted in from third to home. He landed with both feet on home plate before the kids rushed out from the dugout to slap him five, one by one.

"I knew you could do it, I knew you could do it!" Becky gasped, still hopping up and down.

"Would you hush up and sit down? You're making a fool out of yourself."

Becky swung around, stunned to see her sister, Liz, standing behind her. Lizzie's hair had whitened fast. She had it done to a T, in a sparkling silver color that was very attractive, and as usual she was dressed to perfection. She tended to be much happier at social luncheons than she was around the dirt of a ball field. But she was ready for the occasion today. A blue scarf covered her perfect silver waves, and she was actually wearing jeans and sneakers and a Tampa Bay Buccaneers sweatshirt.

"Liz?" Becky said.

"Come sit down, Rebecca. You're screaming like an idiot."

"But he nailed it! Davey nailed it! The damned thing went right over the fence, just like he pointed. He did it, Lizzie, he did it —"

"Of course he did it. He's an exceptional child. Did you expect anything less?" Liz demanded. "I realize the strain of playing Santa may be getting to you —"

"How did you know I was playing Santa?"

"It's a small town. People talk."

"And they talk swiftly!" Becky muttered. "Who told you that?" she demanded.

Liz waved a hand in the air. "Come and sit with me. That's my spot. Right there in the bleachers."

Becky allowed herself to be drawn away from the fence. This last tryout was far from over. Davey ran into the dugout, and another kid came out to bat.

Mike Harden, apparently distraught over Davey's hit, walked this kid. By the next batter, Mike was mad again, and the kid went down quickly. Another batter came up, and his parents screamed for him. Mike Harden's father kept shouting to Mike to strike 'em all out, strike 'em all out. Becky didn't care. Mike and Lew couldn't bother her now.

Davey had just nailed one.

Becky swung around to stare at Liz. "I can't believe that you're on a baseball field," she told her sister frankly. "I didn't even know you knew about these tryouts, or that Davey was trying to make the team —"

"Oh, I do hear things!" Liz said, watching the kids at bat. "Even though you don't keep me informed as to what is going on, I manage to hear things!"

"But how — ?"

"Paige told me that Davey would be on the field this afternoon, and that you'd be here. And that I could get a look at Tim Yeagher up close."

Liz glanced at Becky at last, green eyes sparkling.

"Oh, no." Becky moaned, wondering what fool had told Liz anything at all about Tim. Paige?

"Where are the kids?" Becky asked.

"I'm right here, Mother," Paige said, and Becky twisted to look one row up and saw Paige complacently seated behind her. She had brought her headphones and Walkman. Willing enough to support her cousin —

But not dumb enough to be bored while doing it! Paige grinned and set her headphones in place.

"Where are the boys?" Becky asked. Liz

pointed. Justin and Jacob were in the first row behind the dugout, where they could talk to Davey and the other kids. Becky smiled, suddenly not caring in the least that she'd tap-danced most of the morning, played Santa, and had to come up with thousands of dollars. She spent so damned much time pulling at threads, but today they seemed to have come together. No matter how much the children fought one another at home, they had all shown up — even Lizzie — in support of Davey today. That suddenly mattered more than anything.

Even more than his phenomenal hit.

"Do you know what half the parents here were doing before they came to this ball field?" Lizzie asked conspiratorially.

"What?" Becky had to ask.

"They were shopping at the mall."

"And?"

"There are wonderful, juicy rumors going around these bleachers about you and that ex-jock."

Tim was coming around the fence. The kids were all switching positions. Those who had been in the dugout were coming out. Those who had been in the field were sitting down in their team's lineup.

Davey was running out to third base.

And Tim Yeagher was walking up to see

her, eyes warm and bright, lips curled into a deep, proud smile.

He paused beside Becky's seat on the bleachers. "He did it. The kid really had it in him. He smacked that ball clear out of the playing field, no doubt about it," he told her happily.

Becky lowered her voice. "Was it enough? Will he make the team?"

"There are three coaches. We each pick ten kids. The top ten out of the three lists are the ones who make the team. Davey did well today. So have some of the other kids. We'll just have to see, Becky."

Liz suddenly leaned over. "How do you do, Mr. Yeagher. I'm Liz Larson, Davey's other aunt. I've been dying to meet you, but since Becky doesn't seem to be in a rush to make introductions, I thought I'd best take things into my own hands."

"Ms. Larson," Tim said, taking Liz's offered hand and shaking it, grinning as he looked at Becky. She shook her head sternly in warning.

But she hadn't been prepared. Not for Liz. Not today.

"You do get around, Mr. Yeagher, so I hear."

"Lizzie," Becky warned.

"Just what do you hear, Ms. Larson?" Tim

asked politely, ignoring Becky.

"Why, not an hour ago, you were sitting on my sister's lap in the middle of the mall, asking for special gifts for Christmas!" Liz said, sounding indignant.

"Liz!" Becky moaned.

"Yeah, I *was* at the mall. On your sister's lap," Tim said. "I wanted my Christmas present."

"And what were you asking for?"

"Lizzie, Tim —" Becky said.

"Dinner," Tim said. "I wanted her to come to dinner tonight."

"Dinner!" Liz said. She sniffed. "Where have you been, young man? You should be asking for a lot more than that! This poor girl has been on the shelf for years now!"

"Well, confidentially, I'm trying for more," Tim said, his eyes on Becky, his soft tone for Liz. "All completely aboveboard, of course."

"Oh, no!" Liz said, sounding dismayed. She leaned close to Tim. "Aim for a wild affair at the very least! Although I must admit I heard a really wonderful rumor that you two were involved a while ago. My little sister gave away a whiff of something exciting to one of her reindeer friends. Something to do with tacos in a bathtub —"

"Liz!" Becky gasped. Oh, dear Lord! She

wanted to crawl beneath the bleachers! Who had she told about that one night when the kids had all been out and she had stayed at Tim's?

Julie — that little reindeer rat!

"Tacos in the bathtub!" Becky turned around quickly. Paige had shed her headphones and was smirking away, staring at her mother. *"Tacos?"* Paige shook her head in sad confusion, then muttered, "Ugh." She shuddered. "How messy. I mean, wouldn't you have salsa everywhere — ?"

"Paige!" Becky gasped at her daughter in a strangled tone, her face beet red. They were laughing at her, she thought, her daughter and her sister. And Tim was just standing there, totally unremorseful.

Becky's eyes narrowed at Paige. "We ate neatly!" she gasped. "And now that you've included my impressionable teenage daughter in this —"

"Oh, Mother! Really, I'd never have tacos in a bathtub!"

"Good —"

"Grapes, Mother. Something more sensual, more exotic!"

"Paige!"

"Just kidding, Mother. For the moment, anyway."

Becky let out a soft cry of absolute frustration. "If you will all excuse me, I think I will go see my nephew!"

She leaped from the bleachers and hurried toward the dugout, feeling her back burn from all the eyes staring holes through it. Paige had now heard about tacos in the bathtub, Liz had heard about tacos in the bathtub, in fact, the whole damned town must have somehow heard about tacos in the bathtub. She wanted to die. She wanted to crawl right beneath the fence and into the dirt and die.

But of course, she couldn't do that. The kids out in the field were running in. Those in the dugout were running back out. Becky saw Davey run in and take a seat on the wooden bench just a few feet away from her.

"Hey, kid!" she called softly from the fence at the dugout. Davey turned and stared at her through the square links of fence. He grinned broadly.

"All right!" she told him softly.

"Thanks."

"I always knew you could do it."

"I'm not on the team yet," Davey reminded her.

"Yeah, but boy, Mrs. Wexham, did you see that hit?" asked Billy Simpson, a wiry little platinum blond sitting next to Davey.

She nodded. "Yeah, I saw it."

"He nailed Harden," Billy said happily. "Nailed him good!"

"Yeah, but there's more batting to get through," Davey said.

Becky nodded. "Yeah, and you don't have to kill the ball all the time, Davey. Sometimes just getting to first base is important. It's a team — another kid may have to help bring you home."

"I know all that, Aunt Becky," Davey said very patiently. Becky decided it was time she returned to the bleachers.

She didn't go back and sit beside Liz. She found a place opposite, in the first row.

But Liz found her.

"Gee, I don't get it," Liz said. "Tall, dark, and handsome, and he only wants to take you to dinner? What a hardship! Why, he should just be shot!"

"Liz —"

"Makes a good living, dependable, has a head on his shoulders just the right size, not big at all when it might have been gigantic."

"Liz —"

"What's the matter with dinner, Becky?" Liz smiled wickedly. "You've already had a Mexican meal, it seems. Wasn't — dinner — good?"

Becky sighed and stared at her sister, dumbfounded. "Mexican was great, and another dinner is fine, Lizzie. But when it's over, I have to come home."

"Want some advice from your big sister?"

"No."

"You never did. Take it anyway. Here's the advice — take a chance. Give yourself a real Christmas gift, and take a chance."

"Liz, people get hurt taking chances."

"Yes, and getting hurt is part of living. You're so good with the kids, Becky. Get out there and get up to bat yourself."

Becky groaned.

"Liz, life isn't a baseball game."

"But it is, Becky, sometimes. Sometimes it's all about getting up there and having the courage to take a swing with the bat. Oh!" she cried suddenly. "There — look! Davey is up at bat again."

And he was. Becky inched forward on the seat, holding her breath as the first ball flew by Davey. The ump called it high.

Mike Harden's father called the ump blind.

The next ball flew by.

A strike.

Two more balls. Another strike. Becky was on the edge of her seat.

Let him hit it, God, please, let him hit it. Even if it's just a base run . . .

He did hit it. With a firm whack. The ball

went up and up, and . . .

"Heads up!" a coach roared in warning from the field. Davey had hit a good sound foul ball, and it had flown up and over the bleachers.

"Heads up!" Lizzie cried, and promptly ducked, after slamming her fingers over Becky's eyes.

"Liz!" Becky moaned, freeing herself. Half of the parents had jumped up. Davey's foul ball landed harmlessly on a patch of earth beside the bleachers, and all the smaller children in the area went scrambling to retrieve it.

"Way to stay alive, Davey, way to stay alive!" Billy Simpson shouted from the dugout.

Mike Harden wound up again. He spat, and spat again. He offered Davey his tough-guy-gonna-get-you evil grin.

The ball came flying . . .

And Davey hit it. Hard. A nice, firm, hard whack. The ball grounded toward the second baseman.

"Run, son!" one of the coaches called.

Davey did. With all speed, he came careening toward first. He hit the base a split second before the first baseman caught the ball.

Becky held her breath.

"Safe!" the ump shouted, dramatically throwing his hands out.

"Good hustle, kid! Good hustle!" the coach called.

Becky breathed again and leaned back.

"Davey's going to be all right," Liz said after a moment. "And as to you —"

"Liz!"

"I'll see you on Christmas. Don't be late to church, and don't burn the turkey."

"I never burn the turkey, Liz," Becky said.

"Don't dry it out, then!" Liz said. With a superior smirk, she walked by the dugout, called something to Davey, and proceeded out of the park. Becky watched her go.

A moment later, one of the coaches called the kids into the dugout. Becky watched Tim come back in, speak to the other coach briefly, then address the boys in the dugout. "We've got some great players here," he said. "A lot of talent, and a lot of heart, and sometimes, the heart is just as important as the talent. We're going to call you sometime after Christmas to tell you who's on the team — and who's on the backup list. Every one of you has come far enough now to be backup."

"We're all on the team, coach?" one of the kids asked.

Tim shook his head. "Nine of you will make up the team, and we've decided we'll have three substitutes. And the other three will be backup for those subs, just in case things happen. That sound good and fair to all of you?"

"Yeah, Coach Yeagher!" a hefty dark-haired kid said.

"But why won't you let us know who made it before Christmas?" Mike Harden asked.

Tim stared at him. "Because there are three of us choosing the team."

"What you worried about, Mike?" his father asked, grinning broadly. "I'm the sponsor, and even if I weren't, you're still the best pitcher we've got!"

Mike grinned. Tim looked as if he wanted to punch Coach Harden in the jaw. Both of the statements that Harden had made were true. They didn't need to be drilled into the other kids sitting in the dugouts.

"That's it," Tim said. "You're all winners in my book. Get out of the park and have a great Christmas — all of you."

He walked out of the dugout. For a moment, his eyes met Becky's. Then he walked out of the park, heading for his car, a troop of kids following behind him.

Davey came around the dugout. Jacob, Justin, and Paige all greeting him with hugs.

"You did great, kid," Justin told him.

"For a little butthead, you did more than great!" Jacob said enthusiastically. "You did damned good, you —" he broke off, seeing his mother. "Darned good, darned, darned good!"

"I heard the first one," Becky warned her son.

"Sorry, it slipped out. The heat of the moment. The stress, the excitement —"

"Can it," Becky told him, but she tousled his hair and slipped one arm around Jacob's shoulder and the other around Davey's. She smiled at her nephew. "They're all right. You did just great," Becky said, giving Davey a squeeze. "That was an incredible hit. More incredible than it needed to be, you know, because a base hit can always bring another player in. Remember that. You won't cream them all the time —"

"But he sure creamed that one!" Jacob said, still pleased, as if it had all been his doing. "That practice helped you, huh?"

"You're a good pitcher. Better than Mike Harden," Davey told his cousin.

"Oh, jeez, can we go home now?" Paige begged.

"Yeah," Becky agreed. "Come on, let's get back to the house now."

They started out across the field, Paige carrying Davey's bat, the three boys with their arms linked together.

"Even Aunt Liz was here!" Davey said after a moment, as if he were stunned.

Becky had to admit that she'd been pretty stunned herself. "Even Aunt Liz came. Come on, I've got to get some kind of dinner on."

"You're going out to dinner, Mother," Paige said flatly. "We'll make do on our own."

"Don't be ridiculous. I can —"

"Pizza Hut delivers, Aunt Becky," Davey said firmly. "Don't *try* to tell us you're not going out!"

"Even if I do go out," Becky said firmly, "there's no reason I can't get dinner going first."

"There's lots of reason," Paige said.

"Lots?" Becky asked.

Paige nodded. Justin joined her and plucked something from his mother's hair. "Piece of candy cane," he told her apologetically. "Santa must have been handing out candy."

"You need a nice long shower, or a hot bath," Paige said. "A luxurious shampoo —"

"Perfume!" Jacob volunteered.

"I'll help pick out your outfit," Paige said.

"Whoa!" Becky called.

The kids all stopped. And stared at her, every single one of them.

"All right," she said. "I'm going to dinner. I'll take a long shower, and I'll wear perfume, Jacob. But I'll pick my own outfit."

"Mother, one more thing," Paige said.

"What's that?"

"Don't walk out on your date, and don't come home early!"

Becky sighed and walked ahead.

"Tacos in the bathtub," Paige murmured from behind her. "Didn't these guys ever hear of white wine, or something more romantic, more . . . neat?"

"Paige!" Becky warned.

"Coming, Mother!" Paige said meekly, and Becky heard laughter in her daughter's voice.

It was a hard life, Becky decided. A darned hard life!

Chapter 8

Davey drove back to the house with Aunt Becky and his cousins, but when his aunt headed for the shower and Jacob disappeared into his room and Justin and Paige began to argue in the kitchen over pizza or the rib-runner, Davey sneaked back out.

He hurried to the field, feeling a little bit of December chill in the air. It had been so warm for this time of year.

He'd thought at first that he missed Christmas being white — there had almost always been snow for Christmas when his parents were alive and he had lived up north.

There was no snow in Florida, of course. And he didn't really miss it, he realized. He missed his folks.

Still, the cool air felt good. The weather service had been saying that it might dip all the way into the twenties for Christmas Day. It had actually snowed here a few times, so he had heard. Tim Yeagher had told him that it even snowed in Miami once, but if you blinked at the wrong time, you missed it. Then he had winked, so Davey wasn't really sure if it had snowed in Miami after all.

It just might snow in the Orlando area, though. Little flakes that disappeared right away, he had heard, but little snowflakes nevertheless.

It didn't matter. Snow, no snow — it wasn't even Christmas yet, and he had gotten some great presents. Not the kind that could be wrapped. Presents nonetheless.

He reached the playing field at last. It was so quiet now, when it had recently been so very alive.

Funny, Jacob had always driven him the craziest, but his youngest cousin had been the most supportive this afternoon. He'd been so darned pleased with himself, determined that his helping that morning had made the difference.

Davey hadn't said anything, and he couldn't have said anything anyway. They'd already made fun of him over Babe Ruth. He wasn't going to try to convince anyone again that the Babe had somehow come back to help an awkward kid make a Little League team.

"Miracles!" Davey murmured softly. Christmas miracles. He knew the truth, no matter what his cousins believed. The Babe had helped him. Just like an angel from heaven, the Babe had come and helped him.

And he knew it.

Now, all he wanted to do was say thanks.

"Babe!" he called softly. He looked around. The playing field was empty. The wind rustled slightly, weaving through the nearby trees. Red dirt swirled beneath his feet.

Maybe he was being too pushy.

"Mr. Ruth? Mr. George Herman Ruth?" he called out. *"Babe!"* he exclaimed, saying it a little bit louder. But still there was no reply. The wind continued to blow softly, stirring up the red baseball dirt. The trees rustled in distant conversation, and that was it.

The Babe was gone, so it seemed.

"I wish you'd come back!" Davey said to the air. He kept searching the field. "I wish you'd come back just long enough for me to say thank you. I couldn't have done any of it without you. I don't know if I've made the team or not, but at least I had a good day. You should have seen Mike Harden's face when I hit that ball! It was great. Running the bases was great, getting to home plate was great. I just wish — I just wish that you could have been there."

He fell silent and listened again. He spun around to look into the dugout, then to the empty bleachers. A few paper cups were strewn about — they hadn't quite reached the garbage cans. The wind picked up a gum wrapper and tossed it down again.

Davey stared to left field and then to right.

And still there was no sign of the Babe.

"Thanks," he said again softly to the air. "Thanks so darned much!"

He turned and started home.

Becky settled in for a long spell in the tub, with perfumed bubble bath and the works.

She shampooed all the candy cane out of her hair and scrubbed the very last of the stickum from the false eyebrows, moustache, and beard from her face. She took her time, she doused herself in body powder, and she dressed carefully for dinner, wearing a beautiful white velvet cocktail dress with a scoop neck and lace-edged long sleeves. She hadn't had it on in years; she hadn't known it would still fit. It did. The dancing reindeer job kept her in her old clothes, if nothing else.

She had to admit, meeting her own reflection in the mirror, that she felt good tonight. Dinner. Just dinner. No guarantees, but she did like Tim; no, she was falling in love with him; no, she did love him. She was so afraid to admit that kind of feeling.

Don't admit it, then! she admonished her reflection in the mirror. But have fun.

Take a chance. Have a little bit of fun tonight. . . .

My God, even Lizzie is telling you to let go a little and have fun.

She smiled. She felt good. Her hair felt soft against her face, and she loved the scent of the bubble bath she had used, of the light perfume she wore. She swirled around. The dress was really beautiful. A winter dress, a Christmas dress. She could wear it because the night was so deliciously cool. Everything, for once, seemed perfect.

There was a tap on her door. Paige walked in and looked her up and down critically.

"The cream hose — or beige?" Becky asked her daughter.

"The beige," Paige advised.

Becky agreed. She sat at the foot of her bed and slipped into the beige stockings. She looked up at her daughter, arching a brow. "What?"

"A little more blush."

"I have blush on."

Paige nodded. "All right. All right, then." She stepped back. "You look —"

"Yes?"

Just then, Davey stepped into the room. He grinned from ear to ear and gave her a thumbs-up sign.

"You look great," Paige told her.

Becky stood up and kissed her daughter. She glanced at her watch. "Six-thirty. If you're all sure that you're going to be okay —"

"We flipped a coin. It's pizza," Paige said. "And I made a salad — just so you wouldn't go on a guilt trip over junk food."

Becky nodded. "The money for dinner is —"

"On the table in the entryway," Paige said.

Becky nodded again. "Okay, fine. I'm on my way."

She came down the stairs. Justin and Jacob were waiting in the entry, and Becky spun around for her sons. Justin whistled. Jacob nodded gravely. "Not bad for an older woman," he told her, then grinned and ducked when she reached out to rumple his hair.

"We're going to be all right," Paige said. "Now go!"

Becky gave them each a quick kiss and started out. The kids followed behind her.

Just when she was sliding into the driver's seat of the Volvo, things began to go right to hell.

Jacob, who had been standing just a few feet away, suddenly started to sink. Sink. Yes, sink, right into the ground before her eyes.

She was out of the car in an instant, already on the run, when she heard his cry for help. Justin was tearing toward the spot where his brother had stood as well, crying out as Jacob wavered and fell.

Becky plowed blindly through soaked earth, reaching her son just as Justin did. Some pipe buried deep in the earth must have given out, after some monstrous buildup of water, she realized. The side of the yard was suddenly flooded and giving.

"Get to the front of the house!" she cried, slipping an arm around Jacob and running.

Even as they ran, there was a sudden geyser of water. Earth and water plopped on Becky's arms — and the pristine white velvet dress.

They reached the front of the yard, where Paige and Davey were waiting worriedly. Becky paused, panting, and looked back. The geyser spat one last time, then went still.

Her side yard now looked as if she had just struck oil. It was all black and bubbling.

"I guess we need Mr. Beasely back here," Paige said.

Becky nodded bleakly, staring at her yard, then down at her dress.

She'd felt so good, almost as if miracles could happen. She'd wanted Tim for Christmas; in her heart, he'd been exactly what she wanted.

And tonight, she'd been willing to go to bat. To stand up and take her swings . . .

Ugh. The mud and muck were even in her hair.

"Oh, Mom!" Paige said.

"Go and call Mr. Beasely," Becky said. She sounded ridiculously calm. "Tell him I've been giving him big bucks, and that I want him back out here, fixing this system. Right now. I'm going out, and when I come back, I want my septic tank fixed! You tell him that, Paige."

"Right, Mom!" Paige said quickly.

Then Becky spun around, heading for the Volvo again.

"Where are you going?" Justin called, racing after her.

"I have a date," Becky said. Tim had insisted. She was going to show up at seven o'clock. And when she did . . .

Well, he'd have to understand. One look at her, and he'd know he was much better off without her!

"You can't go like that!" Paige called worriedly. "Mother, wait!"

"Paige, please go call Mr. Beasely. And do something about your brothers. They look like Amazonian muck people!"

"Mom!" Jacob wailed. "So do you!"

"Aunt Becky!" Davey cried.

But Becky was already in the car. She had to get this done, and now, when she could really make Tim understand. She shot out of the driveway, with the children running after her.

It wasn't more than a five-minute drive to Tim's house. Still, she arrived exactly twenty minutes late and rang the bell, standing with her mud-spattered face and dress on his porch.

A second later, the door opened. There was Tim. Handsome, immaculate in a cream sweater and deep blue jeans. He stared at her.

She smiled grimly and walked past him. Into his well-ordered living room with its clean lines, deep-cushioned Chesterfield sofa, fine cherrywood bookshelves, and complete and up-to-date entertainment system.

She almost sat on the Chesterfield, then decided she couldn't do that, even in her present mood, not while she was determined to show him just why things couldn't work, why she didn't care for him too much.

She didn't sit. She stood. Tim had followed her into the living room and now lifted her smudged chin while he stared at her. She waited for him to demand an explanation, to tell her that she was a mess, and demand, in dismay, to know why.

But he didn't make any demands at all. In fact, he didn't seem to have noticed the mud.

He smiled. "You're late," was his only comment.

She threw up her arms. "Yes, I'm late. You see, I'm always late. Something is always happening. Don't you even want to know what the hell happened?"

He nodded. "Sure. If you're willing to tell me."

Tears suddenly welled in her eyes, but she decided she was going to control them. "Damn that Mr. Beasely! I hope a reindeer lands right on his head! No — I hope a reindeer does things right on his head. Beasely supposedly put in a whole new system, and I tap-danced my way through an entire mall to pay for it. But despite my great new 'big bucks' septic system, my yard just now exploded. Jacob nearly sank into a pit of septic mush. I've had it — I've really just had it. Oh. Tim, don't you see? I'm the date from hell. This just doesn't work. It doesn't work! Even when things finally look great, it doesn't work. Davey hits a fantastic homer — but then the pipes explode! Even when things look good, they fall apart. It's a complete mess! No — I'm the mess!"

He stared at her for a long moment and then arched a brow. "Well, I will admit, you are a little bit out of control."

"I'm covered with half my yard!" Becky

exploded. " 'What do you want for Christmas, Becky?' 'Why, septic sand! Tons of it!' Yes, I'm out of control. My older sister is laughing at my love life and seems to know more about it than I do! I think I still have Santa whiskers caught in my teeth. I'm tired, I'm filthy — I'm definitely out of control."

He still just stared at her.

"Haven't you got anything to say?" she demanded.

He turned around and disappeared into one of the bedrooms. He came back a moment later with a big white terry robe. "Guest room is over there," he said softly. He dabbed at the mud on her face. "Go take a bath. I'll be back."

"Tim —" she cried.

But he was gone. She watched the door close and stood in his living room shivering for a moment. Then she got a whiff of herself. She whirled around and walked into the neat — almost never touched — guest room and into the new, beautifully tiled bath with its huge whirlpool tub. She sat down and turned on the jets. The water filled quickly. She eased herself into it. It felt good. He even had bubble bath. She poured some in and nearly had a new disaster when the bubbles rose so high, they nearly filled the room. But the water was hot, the bubbles were clean, and she was just exhausted. She'd been willing to try today, she really had. But her life was just a disaster, and she had to admit it.

She closed her eyes, then heard a tapping at the door. She sat up quickly, gathering the bubbles around her.

The door opened. Tim walked in with a box. She stared at him, and he sat on the rim of the tub, not seeming to notice the bubbles that seeped into his sweater and jeans.

"Feel better?" he asked.

She sighed. "I must smell better. I'm calmer. I mean, I can't believe I came in here ranting like that. Smelling like that!" She inhaled and exhaled slowly. "You've been a good friend. A really good friend. You put up with a lot. But I've got to go home. I pulled Jacob out of the mire and came straight over here. I've never just left the kids like that, I mean with such a disaster going on."

"They're fine, Becky. I just went over to your house. Beasely is already there, and he's assured me it's just a pipe, and that he's replacing it right away, and that there won't be any more 'big bucks' to it. He'll be finished by ten tonight — he's promised me. The kids are going over to your sister's house to clean themselves up. Paige said they'll just sleep over at Liz's tonight."

"Oh!" Becky said. She moaned softly. "Liz is never, never going to let me forget any of this!"

"She seems to be enjoying every minute of it," Tim agreed cheerfully.

Becky leaned her head back against the tub. "I'm sorry," she told him again. "I didn't mean to make such a mess of things, I'm just so —"

"Becky, would you quit being sorry?" he demanded. "You're not the date from hell — you just had a few hellacious things happen to you."

"But, Tim, don't you see? That's the whole point. You shouldn't have to deal with —"

"Becky, I'm not a kid, I've been around. I'm older than you."

"Women age faster."

"We've been through this — men die faster."

"But we fall apart long before we die," she said earnestly.

He shook his head. "Becky, I know that you care about me. Me. Not Davey's coach, not some faded image of a sports hero. You care about me. I want you to care about me *more.*"

She stared at the bubbles. "You don't understand. I care about you too much."

"If you do, care enough to have some faith in me. I'm not shallow."

"I never said you were."

"Becky, you never said such a thing, no. But you assume that I need some unencumbered feather-headed young thing who never has a problem in the world. Becky, no one in the world can explain feelings or emotions. No one says, 'Gee, I ought to fall in love with someone thirty or thirty-one, with no kids, who is perfect, cooks, and likes crossword puzzles.' You meet thirty and perfect, and the chemistry just isn't there. Give me some credit. I ask you out because I want to go out with you. It makes me happy to be with you. Becky, don't you see? The chemistry is there — and the septic tank doesn't matter. And the kids don't matter. I like kids. Especially when you admit I exist and let me talk to them."

He spoke the words softly, as a grin just tugged at his lip. "Davey is an especially great kid."

"But he's not my only responsibility," she protested.

"Becky, I like kids in general. I like yours. I know that kids fight, and that they call each other names, and that they make life rough. They make it real and vivid and special, too. I'm not afraid of your life — can't you see that? What can I do to convince you?" he asked.

She swallowed hard. "I want to be convinced!" she admitted softly. "I want to believe. . . ."

"It's Christmas, Becky. What do you want? Reach for it. Take the chance, take the swing."

She lowered her head, feeling the sweetest sensation of lightheartedness creeping into her. She raised her eyes and tentatively smiled at him.

"What's in the box?" she asked him.

"Tacos," he told her.

She started to laugh. Then she reached out, heedless of all the bubbles and the water, and she put her arms around him and kissed his lips.

"You're a good man, Tim Yeagher. Did anyone ever tell you that?" she whispered.

"I don't mind hearing it," he said. "And yeah, you're right. I am a good man. Don't let me get away."

She grinned.

It wasn't such a bad night after all.

Even if she never was going to hear the end of it from Liz.

Chapter 9

Sunday morning dawned bright and clear. Davey awoke in Aunt Liz's brand-new town house on the lake. He looked across the room. Jacob and Justin were still sleeping, Justin on the bed across from Davey's, Jacob on a sleeping bag between them. Davey closed his eyes, tired, thinking about last night.

Aunt Becky had looked pretty wild when she'd driven off. But then Tim had driven up at just the same time Mr. Beasely did, and though Mr. Beasely had always been polite enough to Aunt Becky, he was more so with Tim, swearing that he'd have things right in a matter of hours. They could have just stayed home.

Tim had offered to take them to his house where they'd find Becky.

Once upon a time, Davey had thought that he was working to bring Tim and Becky together all on his own — and he had been. But his cousins had caught on recently, and now there was a solid, silent conspiracy among them. At Tim's question, they had looked at one another very quickly, and then Paige had answered for the lot of them.

"No," Paige had told Tim very definitely. "We're getting fairly old, you know."

"Right," Justin had said. "Paige and I won't be cluttering up the house much longer."

"What?" Tim asked.

Davey slammed his heel down on his cousin's toe. Justin scowled at Davey.

"Nothing!" he told Tim. But Tim stared at him suspiciously, and Justin sighed. "I just meant that if you liked Mom, there wouldn't be quite so many kids around all the time."

Tim arched a brow. "I don't know why this is such a surprise to everyone — I like kids."

Paige bounced quickly back into the conversation. "Thanks! I just meant that we're really very responsible, and we'll be all right on our own. For a little while. Tonight. I mean, Mother is wonderful —"

"Wonderful. Absolutely wonderful," Jacob said.

Justin slammed on his toe with his heel. Jacob yelped but didn't say another word.

"What are you guys trying to say?" Tim asked, laughing.

Once again, Paige tried with a great deal of dignity to gain control of the conversation. "We could just stay here, except that we won't have water for a while and my brother smells like a water buffalo that's been dead for a decade. But don't you worry about it tonight. We'll just go to my aunt Liz's. She loves this kind of thing."

"You sure that's all right?"

Paige had rolled her eyes, and then she set her hands on Davey's shoulders. "Aunt Liz's is great for a night. I just wouldn't want to live there. Right, Davey?"

"Right," Davey agreed.

"But for a night, it's great," Jacob assured Tim. And so Tim had left them, and Paige had called Aunt Liz, and Liz had come right over and picked them up in her pristine model of last year's new Mercury coupe.

They'd listened to Liz tell them that Becky should get rid of the house, that it was too old, it was a shambles. They'd heard it all before.

In fact, Aunt Liz should have committed it all to Memorex — that way she could just switch on the tape player and not have to bother moving her lips when she gave them the same lecture over and over again.

But Aunt Liz was really all right — her heart was in the right place, at least. Once they'd reached the town house, Liz had quit the lecturing, offering them health food squares and skim milk. She didn't have an Oreo in the house, she'd informed Jacob, and she wouldn't think of having one.

Jacob passed on the health food squares after one bite. So did Davey. They tasted like sawdust. Still, all things considered, the night was going to be all right. Jacob smelled better — that was an improvement in itself. They'd come for the Dial soap, and Aunt Liz had plenty of that.

Later that night, Paige had slipped from her room into the boys' room. "Should we give home a try?" she asked Justin, then looked to both Davey and Jacob. One by one, they had nodded. And very quietly, and by the thin ray of a flashlight, they had dialed their house.

No answer — and then the machine came on. Paige hung up quickly.

"She's still out with him — she must be," Paige said.

"Yeah, but it's early. It's only ten o'clock. Aunt Liz is an early bird all the way around," Justin said glumly.

"Yes, but they've been together for hours now!" Paige said hopefully.

"Unless Mom is home — and dousing in a bathtub," Justin said forlornly.

"I mean, they can't just be having dinner with Aunt Becky wearing half the front yard, can they?" Davey asked.

Justin and Paige looked at each other. "I

don't think so, kid," Justin said, ruffling Davey's hair.

"He'll never ask her out again," Paige moaned.

"Well now, he didn't throw her back in the car and dump her in the front yard," Jacob noted.

"He's too polite to do that."

They all fell silent again.

"What a great Christmas," Jacob said glumly. "My mother, the mud lady. And there can't be any good gifts — not with the septic tank and all."

"Oh, what did you want for Christmas anyway?" Justin taunted angrily. "Sony's My First Razor?"

"Don't worry, Justin," Jacob retorted quickly. "We've still sent for your Black and Decker zit popper!"

"Would you two stop it?" Paige demanded. "Mom will always manage gifts for us, because she always thinks of us first. But we haven't thought about her at all. At least, I admit, I didn't. Not until Davey made me see a few things."

"Yeah, she'll manage something. And she'll smile, and be great, and insist on singing Christmas carols — but now she's not really going to be happy," Justin said. "We should have just sat on her tonight! We should have taken the car keys. She started out looking so wonderful, and after the pipe exploded —"

"She left looking like a drowned chicken!" Jacob finished.

"You can't bodily stop your own mother from doing what she's determined to do!" Paige assured him.

"Maybe we should have shot out the tires," Davey suggested.

They all stared at him.

He'd shrugged uncomfortably. "Well, it worked in *Lethal Weapon III*, you know."

"Good idea, butthead," Justin said. "But none of us has a gun."

They all sat there, depressed, silent.

"We did what we could do," Jacob offered. "If only she hadn't rushed out looking that way . . ."

His voice trailed away. Once again, they were all silent and glum.

Paige sighed. "He's a great guy."

"He's not Dad," Jacob said.

"Nobody's going to be Dad," Justin told him quietly. "Nobody. We can't get our dad back, or Davey's dad back."

"Tim wouldn't try to be somebody else," Paige said, looking at Davey. "He'd never try to be our dad, or Davey's dad. He'd just be himself. And that would be . . ."

"Great," Jacob said.

"For us — and Aunt Becky," Davey said firmly.

"He's sure decent to us," Justin agreed.

"I could charge kids for his autograph," Jacob said. "Ouch!" Paige had pinched him. "Just kidding," Jacob said. "Honest, I was just kidding. And besides — well, it probably doesn't matter much now, huh?"

"We've just got to keep believing," Davey said. They all stared at him. He grinned and shrugged. "Hey! Talk about the impossible! And Christmas presents out of the blue and miracles and all that. I did cream the ball today!"

They all laughed. Jacob punched him lightly on the arm. "Yeah, you did cream that ball."

"Just like Babe Ruth. Pointed to the field and sent it flying," Paige said.

"You knew about that?" Justin asked his sister.

"I know a lot about baseball," she said serenely. "Remember, I am the one who actually hit the ball when we were playing in the yard."

"Then you should know about spitting!" Jacob said.

"It's disgusting."

"It's part of baseball," Davey said. "Mike Harden spits all the time."

"Yeah, and he's a disgusting little runt!"

Paige assured him.

Davey didn't have much of an argument for that.

"But I hit the ball!" he said softly. "Mike Harden's ball. And I hit it so hard, it went flying out of the field. If you believe in it deeply enough, you can make it happen."

"You think we can make Mom and Tim happen?" Jacob asked.

"Only Mom and Tim can do that," Justin said.

"But sometimes grown-ups need a little help," Davey said.

Paige sighed and hugged him. "You did good, Cousin Butthead, real good. I think you helped them, but . . ."

"Now it's up to them," Justin told him.

"It's late," Paige said. "Let's all go to sleep with a few Christmas prayers, huh?" She kissed them all and left the room. Davey said his Christmas prayers, the big one for Aunt Becky, then the smaller one for himself: "And please, God, I know I'm pushing it, but if you could just have the Babe come back one more time so that I could tell him thanks . . ."

Soon after, he fell asleep. And now he awoke because of some very loud noise.

He heard it again. It was Aunt Liz, shouting, laughing.

Davey leaped out of bed and saw that his cousins were doing likewise, all tousled-looking, disoriented, wild. They stared at one another and burst out into the hallway, crashing into Paige. They swore at one another and tore down the stairs to the beautiful, bright white and yellow modern town-house kitchen.

There was nothing wrong with Aunt Liz. She was sitting at the kitchen table, sipping her tea, with the Sunday newspaper spread out before her.

She looked up with surprise when she heard the kids, almost as if she'd forgotten she had them in the house.

"Chickens!" she cried. "Come here! You've got to see this!"

They surged forward. Paige gasped out loud.

There was Aunt Becky, front page, all dressed up as Santa Claus. And there was Tim, sitting on her lap, grinning broadly.

ALL I WANT FOR CHRISTMAS! blazed the headline. Davey quickly scanned the story. It was short and sweet, just a few paragraphs about Christmas in Hampton City, and how the spirit of it all was alive with local actresses like Becky Wexham pitching in to help out Santa and his elves — and legends like Tim Yeagher pitching in to cheer up little kids with his autograph.

It was a heck of a picture. It was charming. It seemed to capture all the spirit and fun of Christmas.

"I love it — oh, I love it!" Liz cooed.

"Mom's not going to love it so much," Paige murmured.

"Maybe we shouldn't show it to her."

"Can you imagine that Tim Yeagher might want *anything* for Christmas?" Jacob said, studying the man on Santa's lap. "I wonder what he asked for."

"Oh, I don't know," Liz said. "When you get to be Tim's age, with Tim's assets, you want things that only Santa — or God — can give. I think I know what he wants for Christmas. I sure hope he gets it. Now, kids, what'll it be for breakfast? Granola and strawberries, or granola and bananas?"

"Orange juice," Jacob said wearily.

An hour later, Becky arrived to pick them up. She came in and told Liz that she'd had coffee and that she'd pass on herbal tea. Then she saw the picture blaring at her from the newspaper at the kitchen table.

"Oh, my God!"

She sank down into a chair and let her head crash against the table. She groaned softly.

"Sure you wouldn't like some nice soothing tea?" Liz suggested.

"Quite!" Becky murmured.

"Umm," Liz teased. "If it weren't eight-thirty on Sunday morning, I'd offer you a nice soothing Scotch and soda."

Becky looked up. All the kids were staring at her. She blushed, and her head crashed back to the table again. "You could skip the soda," she muttered.

"Aunt Becky, it's not that bad!" Davey said.

"Maybe Santa should have been sitting on Tim's lap," Jacob mused. "After all, if Tim were Santa, there are all kinds of things you could ask him for!"

"Maybe Tim was Santa last night," Liz slipped in innocently.

Becky's head rose again. She stared at her sister hard. Then she stood up, her brows still knit, while Liz gave her a smirking smile.

"Let's go, kids. Lizzie says we shouldn't be late to church."

"But we're always late," Jacob began.

"Jacob!" Paige warned.

"Thank you, Liz. Thanks for cleaning them all up and keeping them overnight."

"Don't think a thing of it!" Liz said with a wave of her hand. She slipped an arm around Paige's shoulders. "Jacob was the only one who was actually disgusting, but he is big enough to clean his own ears. The rest of them weren't really bad at all, and they bathed themselves as well. And Becky, you do owe yourself a night now and then." She stopped speaking and grinned at Paige. "And think of it! The man is gainfully employed. At a television station, no less. I mean, she might have been carrying on with another dancing reindeer."

"Liz!" Becky snapped. "There's nothing wrong with dancing reindeer."

"But they are better when limited to one in a family."

"Liz!"

Liz laughed. Becky pushed the newspaper to the far end of the table and started across the room. "Kids, we've really got to go!"

"Did you want me to cut that picture out and frame it for you, dear?" Liz called after Becky.

Becky paused and turned back. "Lizzie," she said sweetly, "you don't really want me to tell you what I think you should do with that paper, do you?"

"Merry Christmas to you, too!" Liz said serenely.

Becky groaned and slammed out of the house.

"Mom, are you all right?" Paige asked when they were all in the car.

"Sure," Becky said.

"Mom —"

"The septic tank should work well now," Becky said.

"Mom!" Paige wailed. "How was your date?"

"Why don't you guys just read about it in the papers?" Becky suggested.

"We tried to. We're just not really sure what we read," Paige told her.

"Neither am I," Becky said. "Neither am I. Anyone for doughnuts after church?"

"Yeah!" Jacob said appreciatively.

"Oh, yeah," Davey echoed him.

Becky frowned at them in the rearview mirror. "Be kind to your aunt. Your best interests are in her heart. And she's right, we've got to acquire better eating habits."

"Right," Jacob agreed.

"But for this morning —" Paige said.

"Doughnuts!" Davey finished.

"But Mom," Paige said again. "What about last night?"

"Mr. Beasely finally fixed the whole system. Without the help of the tree people, I might add. And without more 'big bucks, big bucks.' "

"We don't care about Mr. Beasely," Justin said.

"Yeah, he's bald," Jacob supplied helpfully.

"We want to know about Tim," Paige said.

Becky was silent for a moment. "Tim is a very nice man."

"Wow! It went well!" Jacob cried.

"No, wait!" Justin warned. "He's a nice man, *but* what, Mom?"

Becky sighed. "He's nice, he's great. But you just can't get your hopes set on that — that he'll be around all the time."

"Why not?" Jacob demanded.

"Because —" Becky began, and broke off.

"Because of all of us, right?" Davey said softly.

"No!" Becky exclaimed quickly. She met all their eyes in the rearview mirror. "No, never! And you all listen to me. You're more important to me than anything in the world. Don't ever forget that. You're Christmas every day."

"Even when we're fighting?" Jacob asked.

"All right — so you're Christmas every other day!" Becky said firmly. "Maybe Christmas can't come every day — it wouldn't be so special if it did. Remember, Christmas itself is the miracle! God's day!"

"And God can do anything," Paige reminded her softly.

"But God is really busy," Becky said. "There's famine in Africa, war all over the world!"

"But he hears every prayer," Paige said softly.

"Just like Santa hears every wish," Jacob murmured.

"Guys, Tim is great. He's a good friend."

"It *is* us," Jacob said bleakly.

"No! It's the fact that I'm getting older, that I've had a slice of life already, that —"

"That you've got a house with four kids in it," Paige murmured.

Becky sighed. "Tim *likes* kids."

"You expect us to believe that?" Paige asked her.

"Of course!"

"Then maybe you should believe it yourself," Paige told her very softly.

"Paige —" Becky began, and then fell silent for a moment. Then, to their amazement, she started singing. " 'Deck the halls with boughs of holly' — come on, guys, come on. It's Christmas."

"Mom —" Justin began, but Becky was singing on top of his protest.

"If you want doughnuts," Becky warned, her eyes narrowing. "Sing! Remember, it's Christmas. Get into the damn — darned spirit of the thing!"

So they started to sing. And they were still singing when they got to church.

They pulled into the parking lot just in time.

Becky finally let them quit singing as they hurried out of the car.

"I don't know why we have to come to church today when Christmas is the day after tomorrow," Jacob grumbled. "I mean, couldn't we just get all week in with the one shot?"

"No," Becky told him flatly.

Davey kicked his ankle and whispered quickly, "When you want Christmas miracles, you have to remember to ask nicely — and keep asking, again and again and again!"

"What?" Becky asked, frowning.

Davey brought his finger to his lip and indicated that they had reached the door to the church. He innocently told her, "Shush!"

They all poured in quickly past her, and Becky brought up the rear. They took up more than half a pew.

It was all right. The choir was singing "God Rest Ye Merry, Gentlemen," and the congregation was joining in. The service was nice, and the church felt warm. Davey found himself thinking about what Aunt Liz had said.

At Tim's age, his gifts had to come from Santa — or from God.

Miracles. Christmas miracles. And they could come from very strange Christmas angels — like Babe Ruth.

The congregation left the church singing "Silent Night, Holy Night."

They went for doughnuts, just as Aunt Becky had promised. She told them that she'd bought Aunt Liz a fruit and vegetable dehydrator for Christmas.

They each grabbed another doughnut.

Becky still didn't really say anything at all about her date, or Tim, other than warning them that they mustn't depend on him, and that he was a nice man.

Their mailman was a nice man!

But Aunt Becky was behaving strangely. She didn't complain that Jacob was eating too many doughnuts, and she didn't even seem to notice when he ordered five chocolate ones, the kind she usually considered the worst. She didn't insist they get orange juice or milk to drink — she didn't say a single word when Paige had ordered a diet Coke.

Caffeine free, of course.

Actually, the whole time, Aunt Becky barely said anything at all.

When Davey, Paige, Justin, and Jacob came into the house, they all stared at one another for a moment.

And they waited.

She didn't say a thing about them cleaning their rooms. She didn't remind them that it was almost Christmas, and she didn't say that she needed the parlor vacuumed or could really use an extra pair of hands in the kitchen to peel potatoes.

She was just quiet, ignoring them all. Walked right by them. She wouldn't say anything more about Tim, and yet . . .

She just didn't seem to be all there.

"Mom, you need some help?" Paige asked her.

Becky stared at Paige blankly. "What? Oh, no — um, why don't you go wrap your gifts, or something?" She started up the stairs.

Looking at one another worriedly, the kids all wondered if the last septic explosion hadn't been just one too many.

Chapter 10

It was Christmas Eve at last. Davey stood in the old-fashioned Victorian parlor alone, staring at the tree, at the decorations, and at all the Babe Ruth paraphernalia that Aunt Becky had let him set up in the room. It was pretty wild-looking, he had to admit. But neat. Lots of people lived in the house, he thought. And even though they called each other names now and then, they loved one another. He'd lost his own home, but the substitute he'd gotten was pretty good.

He left the parlor and hurried back up to his own room, digging into his closet to find some of the packages he'd stuffed there.

He hadn't had much chance to earn money this year, but he'd saved up a little from before, and he'd given his gifts a great deal of thought. Some tapes for Paige's Walkman, a new basketball for Justin, and some really good baseball cards for Jacob. He'd even wrapped all the gifts himself — which everyone would probably be able to tell, since he hadn't done such a great job, he thought.

He just didn't have a knack for doing corners.

He had gotten perfume for Aunt Becky. He wanted more for her. And he had really tried, and it had really seemed that things were going so well.

And then the septic tank again. Oh, well, like Aunt Becky had said — such things happen.

But Mr. Beasely had fixed the pipe. Aunt Becky did have a working septic system for Christmas. And that was great, it was just that Davey wanted more for her still.

He picked up his gifts and hurried to the door, wanting to run them down and set them beneath the tree before his cousins reappeared in the parlor. He could hear music playing from Jacob's room, and Paige was talking away on the phone. Aunt Becky was in the kitchen fixing dinner, and Davey was pretty sure that Justin was in with her, carving the meat.

When he came back into the parlor, he started, his eyes very wide.

The Babe was back. Standing right there in the parlor, by the tree, looking around. He seemed pleased with all that he saw, and his smile lit up when he met Davey's eyes.

"Nice place you got here, kid. Real nice place."

"Thanks," Davey said. He walked in and set his gifts down, then turned back to the Babe, a little hesitantly at first. "I tried to reach you the other day. I called to you, but all I heard was the wind."

"Well, I'm here now, kid."

"I wanted to thank you. You were great. Everything you taught me helped. You — you worked a miracle."

The Babe shook his head. "No, kid. You worked the miracle. You worked hard for that hit."

Davey's eyes widened again. "You saw it?"

"Sure did. You pointed straight out to left field, and then you nailed that sucker."

"It still doesn't mean I'm on the team."

"It gave you a good fighting chance."

Davey nodded. "Yeah, it did. I know it sure helped. I don't know if it will do any good for Aunt Becky even if I do make the team —"

"You've done your best, kid. Tried your hardest. Now you have to believe in a few miracles."

Davey grinned. "I believe in miracles. That hit of mine was one."

"They can only come when you believe in them. They're gifts."

"You did so much for me. You've given me so much. You were the greatest Christmas present in the whole world. I don't know how you came to be here —"

"Miracles, Davey."

"I meant to have a great Christmas present for you, I really did —"

"Hey, kid. You don't know much about coaching yet. That hit you made was all the Christmas present I needed. But you know what?"

"What?"

"There still might be an extra-special present under that tree for you."

Davey shook his head. "What could there be?" he asked. "I got what I asked for — you. To help me. It was a great day. Well, until the septic pipe erupted or exploded — or whatever it did! You should have seen the way Aunt Becky went over to Coach Yeagher's house! And she's been so strange since then." He paused, shrugging. "She keeps warning us not to get too attached to the idea of him being around."

The Babe shrugged fatalistically. "Maybe there's not so much to worry about. She ran out of here not looking so great, right? But lots of times people don't care about what other people are wearing."

"Even if it's — mud and — and . . . worse?"

"Mud washes, kid. But who knows? We'll have to wait and see on this one, huh?"

"Sure." Davey nodded. "Sure. Still, I wish —"

"The hit was great," the Babe said. "Like I told you, there was only one thing I ever wanted to do that I didn't get to do, and that was manage a team. I kind of got to manage you. I like coaching. You were a great kid to coach."

"And you were a swell coach," Davey said.

The doorbell rang just then. Davey ignored it for a minute, watching the Babe, hoping that someone would come running down the stairs and see him in the flesh and know that Davey had never been crazy.

But nobody came running down the stairs.

"Will someone please get that?" Aunt Becky called from the kitchen.

"Hey, butthead!" Jacob called from upstairs. "Aren't you down there in the parlor? Can you get the door?"

"Butthead," Davey said, shrugging to the Babe. "That's, uh — that's me."

"Butthead?"

Davey shrugged again. "It's not so bad." He grinned. "I live with Numbnutts, Dimwit, and Idiot, so I guess it's not so bad."

"Oh," the Babe said gravely.

The doorbell rang again.

"I've got to get the door," Davey said. He started out of the room, then turned back.

"Don't go away. Please, stay if you can."

"Ah, kid. It's Christmas. You've got family tonight."

"Please, stay —"

"You'd better get that door," the Babe said.

Davey nodded and hurried into the entryway. Paige was screaming at him now. As he reached the door, he nearly collided with Justin, who had run in from the kitchen, and with both Paige and Jacob, who had run down the stairs.

"What the heck took you so long?" Paige demanded irritably.

"The butthead can hit, but he can't hear!" Jacob said.

"Would somebody answer the damned — darned door?" Justin demanded.

Davey threw it open. They all went dead silent. Tim was standing on their porch with an armful of presents.

He peeked around the packages. "Can I come in?"

"Oh, yeah, yes!" Justin stuttered.

"Let me help you," Jacob told him, reaching for the pile of gifts. He looked up at Tim. "For us?"

"Don't be ridiculous," Paige said serenely. "They're for Aunt Becky."

"No, Paige, there's only one little one in

there for your aunt Becky. The others are for you kids."

"Jeez, wow — thanks!" Jacob said. He stared at Davey with a definite warmth in his eyes. It had been there ever since Jacob had realized that they all wanted the best for his mother. "Hey, Davey, let's take them in under the tree. Let's see what's for who, huh?"

Davey nodded, glad that Jacob had actually called him by his name. But he stared at Tim, amazed that he was here.

"Where's Becky?" Tim asked.

"In the kitchen," they supplied in unison.

But Becky wasn't in the kitchen anymore. She'd heard the commotion in the entryway and come out. There was a smudge of flour on her cheek, but she still looked great, Davey thought. She had an apron over a soft blue sweater-dress, and she seemed surprised to see Tim. She just stood there staring at him.

"I hope you don't mind company," he told her.

"I — no. I expected you on Christmas Day," she told him.

"Yeah. But other people might be around on Christmas Day," he replied. "I wanted to come tonight, when it was just the family. If I'm not intruding."

"Intruding? With that pile of gifts!" Jacob said.

"Jacob!" Paige warned.

Becky sighed, her eyes rolling toward her youngest son. "You're always welcome," she said softly.

"Yeah! Gifts or not!" Jacob said quickly.

Tim was staring at Becky again, and Becky was staring at Tim. Davey stared from one of them to the other. Something inside him seemed to explode like strange, warm, crystal snowflakes. Something was going on here.

"Flour, Mom," Paige said.

Becky rubbed her face. Wrong place. Tim stepped forward and smoothed the white dusting from her face, grinning.

"Well, the ham came out okay, I think. And since we've got sweet potatoes and white potatoes, I made gravy, and I think *it* even came out okay."

"Oh, thank God! Dinner is safe!" Paige breathed.

Davey turned around suddenly and sped into the parlor. He looked around swiftly. As Davey expected, the Babe was gone. The parlor was empty. Something tugged hard inside Davey. He wasn't going to see the Babe again before Christmas. Maybe — maybe he wasn't going to see him again ever.

He swallowed hard. Maybe that was okay, because the Babe would have known that

Davey wasn't going to be alone tonight any longer. His family was with him now. His family . . .

And Tim.

Jacob and Justin piled into the parlor behind Davey with the stack of gifts in their arms. Paige was behind the two of them, and Aunt Becky was coming in, following Tim.

"Tim," Becky said firmly, "you shouldn't have gotten so carried away with gifts."

"Tell her bah, humbug, kids."

They all turned to Becky. "Bah, humbug!"

Becky arched a brow, then fell silent for a moment, her lips a bit pursed.

"Sit!" Tim said, and pulled her down to sit beside him on the couch. "Now," he continued, and he pointed to one of the boxes. "That's for the entire family. Justin, want to open it?"

Justin nodded, and he hurried to the box. And for all his age and maturity, he looked just like a kid as he ripped into the silver wrappings. "What . . . ?" he began, then he jumped up. "Hallelujah! Welcome to the nineties! It's a CD player, guys! A really neat compact disc player with the amps over here, and wow! It's great."

He fell silent and stared across the room at Tim. "Thanks. Really, thanks."

"It goes back," Becky said.

"It stays," Tim insisted.

"Tim —"

"Becky."

"Honest, Mom!" Paige said.

"Please?" Jacob said, very quietly for Jacob.

"Becky, maybe you should open your gift," Tim said, handing her the one really small box in the group.

Becky took the box, staring at Tim, her brows still knit. She ripped off the paper. "Tim, I hope you didn't get extravagant. Something I couldn't possibly match. I . . . oh!"

She had opened the box, but she was the only one who could see inside it.

She stared at Tim, and Tim stared at her. "Oh!" she said again, and tears were welling in her eyes.

"What is it?" Jacob whispered. "Earrings? Emeralds?"

"Emeralds don't make you cry!" Paige whispered back. "Mom, what did he get you?" she demanded.

But Becky hadn't seemed to hear her daughter. "I — I don't — oh, Tim, this isn't fair! The kids —"

"The kids are exactly why, Becky," he said softly. "You're always so concerned about them. So maybe they should have a say in this, too, huh?"

"A say in what?" Jacob bellowed.

Tim stared at Jacob. "It's a diamond. I want her to marry me."

"A what?" Paige shrieked, jumping up.

"You want to marry —" Justin began.

"Me?" Becky whispered.

Tim took the box from her and took the ring from it. Paige gasped. "Oh, Mom, that rock's a big sucker!"

"Paige!" Jacob said, and elbowed her in the ribs.

"Oh, you stop it, you little —"

"You're sure you want to marry me?" Becky asked over the din.

He took the ring from the box and took her hand, ready to slip it onto her finger. "Well?" he asked softly.

She was still silent, just staring at him.

"Aunt Becky!" Davey cried.

"Mom!" the others shouted in unison.

"Becky, will you marry me?" Tim persisted.

"Oh, God, yes!" Becky cried at last. "I mean, if you're sure, really sure, if you're really totally certain —"

"Becky, I'm sure. I'm certain."

Becky still just sat there, staring at him.

Tim slipped the ring onto her finger.

"Kiss her, Tim!" Jacob cried. "Mom, kiss him! Don't people your age know how to do anything right?"

"Jacob!" Paige, Justin, and Davey elbowed him all at once. He squeaked out with a cry of protest.

"He does do it just right!" Paige said. "Oh, dear Lord, will you look at that ring!"

"Hey!" Tim said, giving Jacob a good warning stare. "I know how to do it all just right. Promise. What do you think, Becky?"

He stood up, pulled her up to her feet, then swept her into his arms and down into a swashbuckling kiss that would have done Robin Hood proud.

They all cheered.

The kiss took off slowly, but it was a darned good one.

Tim's back had to be better than his knee for him to hold her like that so long, Davey thought.

And then he had to wonder if Aunt Becky was even breathing.

Finally, Tim lifted his lips from hers. Becky turned to them all, a little dazed. "Honest. He does it all just right!" she said.

Davey stared at the two of them, unable to believe that even Christmas could be so good.

He suddenly smelled something burning.

"Aunt Becky, what's in the oven?" he asked.

"The rolls!" she cried, and went tearing from the parlor and through the foyer and into the kitchen. And everyone piled in behind her. Smoke was billowing from the stove as she threw open the door and grabbed the tray of pitch-black rolls with her kitchen-mitted hands.

She set them on the counter. "Sorry, guys! I think they're a little overdone."

"I think they're incinerated!" Jacob said.

"And I think they're just rolls," Tim stated. He pulled Becky into his arms and kissed her again.

The kids stared at them for a moment.

"Let's go open our gifts," Jacob said.

"Think we should leave them?" Paige asked.

"Think they'll notice?" Jacob replied.

They all turned and headed back into the parlor and started opening their gifts.

It was great. Paige, Justin, and Jacob all liked the presents Davey had picked out for them. And Davey had gotten some super presents in return. A great leather glove from Aunt Becky, a batting glove from Paige. Justin and Jacob had gone in together to buy him a good pair of cleats. Everyone got excited about the gifts, and one by one, they walked back into the kitchen to show them all to Aunt Becky and Tim — whether they were kissing or not.

Davey found himself alone with the Christmas tree again. "Babe?" he called softly.

But the Babe had gone. No one answered his call.

He collected his things and was about to walk into the kitchen himself when he saw that there was another package under the tree. Probably one for Aunt Becky from one of his cousins, he thought.

He set his stuff down and walked over to the tree. He bent and picked up the package. It was a square box, nicely wrapped.

It was addressed to him. It didn't say that it was from Aunt Becky, or Tim, or any of his cousins, or even Santa. It just had his name printed on it.

He pulled off the ribbon and ripped the paper. It was a box. He opened the box.

And there, carefully preserved in a hard plastic frame, was a baseball card.

Not just any card.

It was a signed Babe Ruth card. The Babe was in his Yankee uniform. His bat was raised high . . .

He had that look in his eye. A look like he could hit anything out there — just because he was so determined to swing at it.

And his signature was on it.

"Wow!" Davey shrieked. He forgot his other gifts and went flying into the kitchen, throwing his arms around Becky and nearly knocking Tim over.

"Thank you, oh, thank you! You should never have done it, really, you should never have done it!"

"Done what?" Becky demanded, staring at Tim over Davey's head.

"The Babe Ruth card, Aunt Becky!"

"What Babe Ruth card?" She took it from his hands, studied it, then stared at Tim.

"Tim!" she cried in dismay. "You still can't be so extravagant —"

"What extravagant?" Tim demanded. "I bought him time at the batting cages for Christmas!"

Becky thrust the card beneath his nose. Tim took it with curiosity and studied it.

"It's real, authentic?" Davey whispered.

"It's real," Tim said.

"Tim!" Becky said again.

"Becky, I didn't do it. Honest, I didn't do it."

"Maybe . . . Santa?" Jacob said incredulously.

"Tim, you're a liar," Aunt Becky charged him, but there was no anger in her voice or her eyes. She walked toward him, the wooden spoon for the potatoes in her hands. "A liar. But a darned good man!" she said softly.

They kissed again.

Davey clasped the card to his chest and

wandered back out to the parlor. He stared at the tree and closed his eyes and opened them again.

But the Babe didn't come back.

"Thanks!" Davey said softly.

He heard Paige shrieking. She came running into the parlor. "It's — it's snowing!" she gasped.

"It can't snow, it's Florida."

"It's snowed before, so I've heard. And I don't care! It's snowing now. Miss it, butthead, or get your buns in gear!"

He set his card down on the table and raced outside with Paige. Jacob and Justin were already out there, swirling around in the tiny flakes.

It wasn't real snow, not the kind he knew, heavy snow that fell and carpeted the ground. This stuff melted when it hit the ground; you couldn't see it at all anymore.

But it was falling from the sky . . .

Little tiny white flakes . . .

Falling and falling.

They all played in it, whirled in it. They shouted to their neighbors, and their neighbors shouted back, and everyone knew that the Florida snowfall would make the newspapers across the country for Christmas morning.

Tim and Aunt Becky stood on the porch,

watching them all whirl around and play, laughing.

His arms were around her. She leaned back against him. There were still stars in her eyes.

After a while, the snow stopped. They came inside, shivering, and they all had hot chocolate with their Christmas Eve dinner.

Afterward, Davey was clearing up the table when the phone rang. Aunt Becky called for someone to answer it, and Tim obliged her.

Just as if he were at home.

Davey smiled at the thought. It would be Tim's home, soon.

"Davey!"

Tim called his name. Davey started for the parlor, but Tim had already walked into the dining room to find him. "Davey, that was one of the other coaches!" Tim said, pleased. "He wasn't supposed to let you know yet, but he knew what it meant to you — and that it was almost Christmas. Davey, you made the team. Not as a sub — you made the top nine." He walked over and picked Davey up, swinging him around. Davey had his arms around Tim's neck and hugged him in return.

Then Tim set him down and studied him hard.

"You're not that excited," Tim said.

"Oh, yes, I am!" Davey assured him.

But Tim's mouth curled into a subtle smile

as he studied Davey, and that smile deepened.

He stroked Davey's cheek, lifting his chin, "The team didn't really mean all that much to you, did it? It was Becky you were worried about, right? And me?"

"Oh, no, coach! I love baseball —"

"I won't tell Becky if you won't," Tim said.

Davey grinned in return.

Tim turned around and left him, and a minute later, Davey heard them cleaning up together in the kitchen.

Much later that night, Davey lay in his bed in his room. The light was out, but the nightlight from the hall cast a glow into the room by which he could just see the Babe Ruth poster on his wall.

"Thanks!" he said aloud softly. "Thanks."

A Babe Ruth card. Snow. And Tim for Aunt Becky.

It was the best Christmas ever.

He closed his eyes, murmuring his prayers. And once again, he thanked God for the Babe Ruth card, and the snow. And Tim.

And Christmas magic, and miracles.

Christmas Day was even better than Christmas Eve. Tim came to take them to church.

He insisted on showing Becky's ring to everyone, and people they barely even knew were all excited.

Becky herself felt as if she were riding on clouds. All night long she had moved her fingers over the ring, feeling the cut and not caring at all that it was a beautiful, wonderful ring, just marveling that Tim really wanted the rest of his life with her. She'd been so afraid that she would awaken in the morning and find out that it had been a Christmas dream.

But when she awoke, the ring had still been on her finger.

And Davey's Babe Ruth card had still been on the mantel. Honestly! Tim was still denying that he had gone out and bought the darned thing!

She'd barely gotten the coffee on before Tim arrived to spend the day with them.

She couldn't wait to see Lizzie's face! But Lizzie would probably think it was all her own doing.

She left church that morning with the kids walking ahead of her and Tim right behind her, his hand at the small of her back as he escorted her out. It felt so good, so warm. One of the little things that meant so much.

"How about doughnuts on the way home, even if it is Christmas?" Tim suggested. "The Donut Hole is open this morning."

"We just had doughnuts the other morning —" Becky began.

"Mom! Lighten up. It's Christmas. And you're starting to sound like Aunt Lizzie!" Jacob warned.

"I resent that!" they heard.

Lizzie was standing behind them.

"I want to see this rock that the entire world has seen already," she said, and took Becky's hand. She nodded gravely, then kissed Tim. Her eyes were sparkling wildly. "Well, at last!" she told Becky, and she did seem smug — just as if she had planned the whole thing.

"And now, Tim Yeagher, does this mean that my sister doesn't have to play an oversize tomato anymore?"

Tim's lip curled slowly as he looked at Becky. "It means that she can be a tomato when she really wants to be one, but that she doesn't have to be a tomato anymore when she doesn't want to be one. A tomato is really a very respectable thing to be, Lizzie."

Lizzie sniffed.

"I always really liked the dancing reindeer costume," Tim assured Becky. "I'm not so sure I ever saw the tomato costume."

Lizzie sniffed again.

Becky laughed. It didn't matter. It was Christmas.

"Doughnuts, anyone?" Lizzie asked, pulling on her gloves, since the Christmas Day temperature was still a remarkable thirty-something. "Becky is doing the turkey, so I'm buying!"

"All right!" Jacob declared.

They headed out of the church again. The others were just a little bit ahead of Becky. She hurried to catch up with them and brushed past a big man in a heavy coat.

She turned around quickly to apologize. "Sorry!" she said swiftly.

He was wearing a wool cap, kind of like a baseball cap. He was a big man, tall, with rounded cheeks, bright little eyes, and a quick smile.

"It was nothing, ma'am. Nothing. Merry Christmas."

"Merry Christmas," Becky said, staring at him. He passed her by, and she hurried from the church, curious. She hadn't seen him before, and yet she had.

She found Tim waiting for her in the parking lot while the others bundled into the cars.

"I'm sorry, I just bumped into a man —"

"A man?" he teased.

She grinned. "And he looked like someone I knew, but I know I don't know him. He looked just like —" She broke off, her eyes widening. "Davey's poster! His new card. That new card you bought him."

"I didn't buy him a card, Becky."

"Babe Ruth! I swear, Tim! He looked just like Babe Ruth!"

Tim grinned. "Elvis is supposed to appear now and then, but not Babe Ruth!"

Becky grinned. "All right, I know he's gone, but — boy, that sure did look like him. I wish Davey could have seen him."

Tim kissed her forehead. "You've got Babe Ruth on your mind."

She shook her head. "I've got *you* on my mind."

"Merry Christmas, Becky."

"Oh, Tim! Merry Christmas!"

He kissed her quickly and led her to his car, since Paige was driving the Volvo.

Becky slid into her passenger's seat. She looked back. The man had come out of the church.

He waved to her.

"Tim —" she began, and turned to wave back. But the man was gone.

"Yeah, Becky?"

He slid into the driver's seat. She took his hand and squeezed it.

"Merry Christmas!" she said again softly.

"A new septic tank and me! What more could you ask for?" he teased.

"Nothing," she said. "Nothing in this world."

Except, she added silently, a baseball team for Davey. And a Babe Ruth card.

And somehow they had gotten it all.

She turned back to the church.

It sure had *looked* like Babe Ruth.

After all . . .

This Christmas had been filled with miracles.

Epilogue

The team was a good one. The sponsor had decided they should be called the Sharks, and so they were.

They won most of the games; they lost a few. Mostly they won, not because Mike Harden was such a good pitcher, or because Billy Simpson could hit so well, or because Davey had learned he could do a phenomenal job running the bases.

They won because they played like a team.

And that was Tim's doing.

The other coaches showed up only for their own team's games, but Tim made every practice. He had managed to make Mike realize that some players were going to hit his balls — and that he had to depend on his basemen and outfielders to catch those balls. Mike finally recognized that his arm could get tired. They all practiced picking the runners off the bases, and they were darned good at it. They even had a few really great double plays.

In the end, they were so good that they reached the state championships.

Even Tim, who always managed to be so level, was excited. The championship game was to be played the last Saturday in May. They practiced for it, they talked long and hard and earnestly, and they practiced some more.

But then the big day came. Tim was up at the crack of dawn — Davey knew because he'd married Aunt Becky on the first day of February and had been living in the old Victorian house ever since. Things had changed subtly since then.

Dinner was usually good. They both liked to cook, and with two people in the kitchen, fewer meat loafs were burned.

Meat loaf, however, did not improve itself.

Aunt Becky was sometimes calmer, and sometimes a little more frenetic. She'd found out just a week ago that she was going to have a baby.

Paige had been somewhat embarrassed, considering her mother far too old for such things.

Aunt Becky considered herself rather old for such things, too. She seemed a little bit in shock, as if the fact that she was going to have another baby was as astounding as the fact that Davey had made a grand-slam home run just when it was needed most.

Tim thought it was great, assuring both

Paige and Becky that they needed another girl to kind of even out the household, but Justin was quick to assure his sister that the chances were fifty-fifty it would be another boy.

In fact, the baby enthusiasm hadn't died down a bit — until the morning of the championships. And that morning, Tim got up early, made coffee, and paced the kitchen.

Davey found him there, walking around in his bathrobe.

"Fired up?" Tim asked him.

Davey grinned and nodded. "But you know what, coach?"

"What?" Tim asked him.

"It's just another game. That's what you always tell us. Playing your best for yourself is what matters."

Tim ran his fingers through his hair. "Is that what I always say?"

"Yep."

Tim grinned. "Another game. You're right, Davey. It's just another game."

But it must have been an important game for him because he was nervous.

He was so nervous that he tripped down the porch stairs when he went out to get the paper.

The next thing Davey knew, he and Aunt Becky were driving Tim into the hospital, and Tim was saying Becky was making a big fuss out of nothing, but two hours later Tim's ankle was all wrapped up and Tim himself was on crutches.

"One of the other fathers will manage!" Becky assured him firmly.

"I have to be there —"

"We'll be there," Becky assured him.

Davey gave her a worried look. Becky frowned, her look asking him just what she was supposed to do.

They still arrived at the field early. And despite Becky, Tim hobbled around, muttering that he wasn't sure about who he should be turning *his* team over to. Mike Harden's father played hard — and went for throats.

His own players', as well as the opponents'.

Coach Mac was just the opposite. A pussycat.

Pussycat coaches just didn't make it.

It was while Davey was sitting in the bleachers, listening to Tim with a sinking feeling, that he looked up and across the field.

His heart suddenly seemed to leap into his throat.

Davey had never thought he would see him again, but there he was, at the Coke stand, just buying a soda. Babe. The Babe. The great Babe Ruth himself, sliding back into Davey's life just when he was needed most.

"I've got a coach!" Davey cried. "Tim, I've

got a coach. The perfect *manager!*"

He leaped up and went running across the field, half afraid that the Babe would disappear before he got there.

But the Babe stood waiting.

Davey rushed up and hugged him, his arms just going around the Babe's girth.

"Hey, kid! I heard it was the big day. I had to come back and see how you were doing," the Babe told him.

Davey looked up at him. "We need you. We need you badly. Tim has sprained his ankle and can't stand on it. Can you manage us for a day, coach?"

"Me? Manage?" the Babe asked. He sounded doubtful but pleased.

"I've told Tim. I told him I had a great coach. You — you aren't going to disappear on me or anything, are you?"

"When I'm finally getting my chance to manage? Not on your life, kid. Not on your life! But you'd better think of some way to introduce me, or else you'll have grown-ups just passing out all over."

"You can be Chris. Like in Christmas," Davey said, grinning.

So the Babe, just as pleased as he could be, allowed Davey to drag him back to the dugout where Tim was sitting miserably in between two equipment duffel bags. Tim looked up.

He looked startled, staring at the Babe.

"I told you. I've got a coach —" Davey began.

"Name's Chris," the Babe said. "Glad to be of service."

"Chris," Tim said, still staring rather blankly. He seemed to give himself a mental shake. He took the hand the Babe offered him and shook it quickly, but he couldn't tear his eyes away from the Babe. "Chris, you must get this all the time, but you sure do look a lot like Babe Ruth."

The Babe laughed. "Yeah, you're right. I hear it all the time. People think I should work for one of those places that sends out pretend celebrities, so I guess I really do look like Babe Ruth. Hope that's enough to get you to trust me with this game."

Tim stared at Davey, frowning. "I really don't know —"

"I do. Tim, please! I know he can make us win!" Davey begged.

"Davey, you don't understand," Tim began. But he broke off when he saw the pleading in Davey's eyes. "We have other fathers who could step in."

"Tim, please! I know Chris can make us win."

Tim threw up his hands. "The team is yours, then, Chris. I'll be here in the dugout.

I'll give you whatever help I can. And Becky's keeping score. She'll be here any minute; she can help keep them in batting order for you."

"Much obliged," the Babe said. "Davey, let's get that equipment out!"

They did. The other kids began to arrive. They all stared at "Chris," but they hopped to as he sent them out to the field to practice, running hard, dropping down to the ground to do a few warm-up push-ups. Then "Chris" began to send balls flying high and low out into the field for the boys to catch. After a while, their new manager called them into the dugout for their pep talk. "Simpson — you make great catches," he began, and found something uplifting to say to each kid on the team, telling Mike he had a great pitch, and that he had a great catcher and great backup, and he just needed to remember it. He smiled at Davey. "And you, kid! You've got heart, and you've got hustle! Everybody's got something special to give, guys. Every one of you has his talent. Use it. Listen to your coaches, and play your best!"

The other team arrived, along with the parents, relations, and friends who came in greater numbers as the game time neared. "Chris" met other parents. He got a lot of wide-eyed stares. He winked at Davey. He smiled a lot.

Moms and dads told Chris that he sure did resemble Babe Ruth. Now and then, of course, there was a parent who hadn't the faintest idea of what Babe Ruth had looked like, so those parents didn't give him a hard time at all.

Then it was game time.

And it was quickly neck and neck.

The Sharks were good, so were the Tigers, a team that had made the grade right out of Miami. Boy, could they hit!

At Davey's first up, he looked at the Babe. The Babe touched his ears and his nose — his sign to let the first one go. Davey did. It was high. The next ball, the Babe nodded and stroked his chin. Davey went for the hit; he fouled, and then, with a one-one count on him, he got the sign to watch the ball and choose himself.

He was walked, which was okay. Mike Harden came up to bat next, and he made a great hit that brought him to second base — and Davey home.

It was a really great game. Tim was stationary, lodged in the dugout, but Becky could move and she was doing so, just like a tiger in a cage. Every time a kid got up to bat, she strained with him. Every time a kid hit the ball, she paced the dugout — as if she could run with him.

Parents were screaming.

Mike Harden's father was promising them all bucks for any hits they got.

Everyone was a coach. A constant barrage of advice came from the bleachers, from mothers and fathers, sisters, and brothers, and cousins alike.

"You can do it!"

"Keep your bat level!"

"Choke up, choke up!"

"You just need one!"

Seven innings made up the game. Davey's team was the home team, so the Tigers were first up to bat each inning, as the visitors. At the beginning of the seventh inning, the score was tied, three to three. This would be the Tigers' last at bat. With the score tied, someone had to come home, or they'd go into extra innings.

Mike Harden was pitching, but his arm was tiring. Davey was playing second base. The Tigers' first batter ended up on first base, walked. The Babe called for time.

"Feeling the strain, huh, Mike?"

Mike rolled his arm. "Yeah, a little."

"Want to be replaced?"

"Wow, coach, I'd sure like to see it out."

"Okay. We'll give it a try. Get this guy out on second. He's going to make a run for it. Watch him good, let a pitch fly straight into your catcher's hand. Got it?"

Mike nodded. A few seconds later, they made the play. Mike skyrocketed the ball to their catcher, the catcher sent it sailing straight into Davey's mitt at second. One out. Mike got such a boost from the out that he managed to strike out the next batter.

But the next man hit a grounder and made it to first. Then the next player was walked. Things were beginning to look desperate.

The next kid came up and hit the ball. It was a beauty. It sailed and sailed. It looked like it would sail forever.

Amazingly, their outfielder caught it. It should have been on film, Davey thought. It was an incredible catch for a kid.

For anyone.

The Sharks cheered and came running in. The Babe was worried, though.

He gave his team another pep talk, stalking the dugout, talking to each player.

"We've got to get up there and do it now. Mike is our best, and our best is tired. It's harder to pitch ball after ball than it is to go to bat once every ninth man. Believe me, I know. Give it your all, guys. Nothing has to be showy. Base hits are good; walks are good. Grand-slam home runs are great, but getting around the bases is what matters, right? Remember, you're a team. Go get 'em."

And they tried. Davey watched Mike

take his turn at bat.

He watched Mike take three strikes, and sit, dejected.

"Pizza after the game no matter what!" Tim called firmly. "Win or lose, you guys have played great, and you've come a long, long way."

Mike looked up and had the grace to grin.

Billy took his turn. A strike. A ball. A strike. A ball. They were all barely breathing.

Another strike. And Billy was down.

"Davey, it's you."

The Babe had called him. Tim was looking at him. He gave Davey a thumbs-up sign.

"Davey, come see me for just a minute now," said the Babe.

Davey trotted out of the dugout where the Babe was waiting.

"Who's that kid after you, Davey? Jimmy, huh? He hasn't had much luck up at bat."

Davey shrugged. "He's our weakest batter. But boy, he can catch just about anything."

"Right. Good kid, good little player. And maybe he's got a chance. You keep batting just the same — you do your best. And don't forget it's important just to get on base. But once you're on base — well, you take whatever chances you have to in order to get around, okay?"

"You sure I can get on base?"

"I'm not sure of anything, kid! But get on out there — make me proud!"

Davey smiled and gripped his bat and trotted on out to the batter's box.

"Watch me, Davey, watch me!" the Babe warned.

Davey nodded and took a good look at the opposing pitcher.

The kid spat.

And then spat again. Davey waited, barely blinking.

The Babe gave Davey the sign to let the first one go. Davey did so. It was called a ball.

But the next one was a strike.

A ball. A strike.

A ball.

Full count. Last inning. The entire game rested on his shoulders.

The pitcher, a tall lanky kid who could move like lightning, wound up for his pitch.

And it came sailing, heading right over home plate.

Davey swung. Hard, level — even. He heard the whack. The ball had connected.

He dropped his bat and ran. It hadn't been one of those point-to-left-field-and-it's-out-of-the-park balls. It had been a grounder, but it was a hard one. They'd really needed a good one, a solid one, an out-of-the-park one. But it didn't matter. Playing mattered, giving it his all mattered.

At least he'd hit the darned thing. And he could hear screaming. And above it all, he could hear a voice: "Run, Davey, kid, keep running!"

The coach's voice. The Babe's voice. Or maybe it was just one that echoed inside his head while the parents beat their feet against the grandstand.

He rounded first just as the ball came sailing to the first baseman.

It was an overthrow. The outfielder who had picked up the grounder had overestimated, and the ball sailed clean over the first baseman's head.

"Run!" Davey heard. This time it was Tim. And he could hear Aunt Becky screaming right along with him: "Run, Davey, run! You can do it."

And he could. He doubled up, went flying off first and dove onto second base, just seconds before the ball landed in the second baseman's hand. But when the second baseman bent down to tag Davey, he dropped the ball.

And Davey was up.

Running. Running had always been his strength. He could move around the bases, and he knew it. The second baseman was going to send the ball to the third in a flash, he knew. But he knew, even as he ran, that the other team was reeling a little bit — a grounder that should have been no more than a base hit was taking him around the field.

The ball hit the ground just three steps from third base. Davey watched it land, watched the stocky third baseman try to keep his body on base while retrieving it. The third baseman couldn't quite do it. He wasn't going to make it, he was going to be just a few seconds short. . . .

So Davey ran.

The catcher, standing off base, stared at Davey with glittering hazel eyes from out of his helmet. "Run him down, run him down!" he shouted to the third baseman.

The third baseman threw the ball to the catcher, and Davey started back to third base.

But then the catcher threw the ball back to the third baseman, and Davey instinctively started back toward home.

The third baseman threw the ball again; then the catcher. Davey kept moving. They were closing in on him.

The crowd was going absolutely wild. Shrieking and screaming.

Mothers and fathers were even running

along, outside the baseline, as if they could move for him.

Wow. Well, it was Little League.

The catcher threw the ball to the third baseman. The third baseman threw it back. The catcher threw it back to the third baseman. They were almost close enough to tag him.

Then Davey got his break.

Third baseman to catcher. And the catcher had to run three steps outside the baseline toward the dugout to reach the ball. It wasn't much, but Davey knew it was all he was going to get.

Davey tore past the kid, no more than a foot ahead of him. The catcher was good. He was right behind Davey. Davey could hear the wild shouting that echoed throughout the entire park.

Home plate. Right in front of him. *Miraculously,* the catcher just a breath behind him. He made a dive, a wild dive, sliding. Fingers stretching out, grasping, reaching . . .

Touching home plate.

"Safe!" the ump shouted.

He was covered in baseball dust from head to toe — he was eating the stuff. He didn't care. His entire team came pouring out of the dugout, lifting him up out of the dirt. He was whirling, spinning — being downright slammed on the back. He looked around quickly. "Coach! Coach — Babe — I mean, Chris! Hey, coach, we did it!"

But there was no answer.

The Babe was gone. Somehow, Davey had known he would be. And the idea made him sad, and yet he was grateful still. He'd gotten so much more than he had ever dared hope!

Davey knew that the Babe had been around just as long as he was needed. And maybe just long enough to touch a dream himself.

The Babe was gone.

But Tim was there, up on one crutch, leaning on Aunt Becky's shoulder. And Aunt Becky was watching Davey with a massive smile and tears making her eyes glitter.

She wasn't going to rush over and hug him or anything — not with all the guys around — even if she wanted to. But she saw him looking for her, and she lifted a thumbs-up sign to him, and he knew that she was as proud of him as anybody could be. Her smile was ear to ear.

Justin was suddenly behind him, slamming his back with his palm, squeezing him up off the ground. Jacob was there, shouting, laughing, and Paige was there, too, ready to give him a good thump. The other coaches came, and even the tall, lanky pitcher from the other team came over. "Hey, Larson, heck of a hustle!"

"Thanks!" he cried back. He wound up on somebody's shoulders, and he found himself looking at Aunt Becky again. She was still smiling, and he smiled himself.

Maybe they'd both learned a few things about baseball — and life.

You just kept swinging, no matter what. And sometimes things didn't go so well. There were strikes and fouls and those darned pop-up flies.

But sometimes, you got a really good whack at things. And if you just kept swinging, and believing . . .

Sometimes . . .

Well, sometimes it was Christmas. Even on the last Saturday in May.

The employees of THORNDIKE PRESS hope you have enjoyed this Large Print book. All our Large Print books are designed for easy reading — and they're made to last.

Other Thorndike Large Print books are available at your library, through selected bookstores, or directly from us. Suggestions for books you would like to see in Large Print are always welcome.

For more information about current and upcoming titles, please call or mail your name and address to:

THORNDIKE PRESS
PO Box 159
Thorndike, Maine 04986
800/223-6121
207/948-2962